UNEXPECTED

UNEXPECTED

Robin wants the leprechaun's treasure. Magnus wants a new job. Keane wants a new life. Connell wants to change the past. Rhea wants a new coat. What these diverse individuals find instead, however, is love and passion that will forever change their lives.

Sometimes, love is best when it's unexpected.

Previously available only in electronic format, these steamy stories of erotic romance by award-winning author Megan Hart have now been combined—due to popular demand—for a paperback edition!

Included are the tales…

Amidst A Crowd Of Stars
Emerald Isle
Everything Counts
Moonlight Madness
Monster In The Closet

PRAISE FOR MEGAN HART

Moonlight Madness

"…A short and dark erotic romance. Discovering why the coat was different is a bit shocking. Rhea then understands what is different about the coat but is intent on keeping it. For me this story is not normally something I would read, but I found it enlightening and freaky and I really enjoyed it."

—Sheryl, *Coffee Time Romance*

"…Grabs you from the beginning and doesn't let go…"

—Kay Smith, *Just Erotic Romance Reviews*

"4 1/2 Hearts!…The twist at the end will take the reader by surprise and is something you would never expect. Megan Hart has done a great job of pulling the reader in and then shocking them with the ending."

—Angel Brewer, *The Romance Studio*

Monster In The Closet

"…A good read. Ms. Hart's story weaving is sensual and sexual. You have to continue reading to find out if Tessa and Magnus are able to accomplish their objectives. I am looking forward to reading more books by Megan Hart."

—Lynn, *Coffee Time Romance*

ALSO BY MEGAN HART

A Siege Of Herons
After Class
All You Can Eat
Always You
An Exaltation Of Larks
Convicted
Dream Upon Waking
Driven
Friendly Fire
From Distant Shores
Lonesome Bride
Love Match
Love Me Two Times
Nothing In Common
Opening The Door
Passion Model
Playing The Game
Pot Of Gold
Right To Remain
Riverboat Bride
Sand Castle
The Clear Cold Light Of Morning
Trial By Fire
White Wedding
Wish List
With Steps Like Knives

UNEXPECTED

BY

MEGAN HART

AMBER QUILL PRESS, LLC
http://www.amberquill.com

UNEXPECTED
AN AMBER QUILL PRESS BOOK

This book is a work of fiction. All names, characters, locations, and incidents are products of the author's imagination, or have been used fictitiously. Any resemblance to actual persons living or dead, locales, or events is entirely coincidental.

Amber Quill Press, LLC
http://www.amberquill.com

All rights reserved.
No portion of this book may be transmitted or reproduced in any form, or by any means, without permission in writing from the publisher, with the exception of brief excerpts used for the purposes of review.

Copyright © 2006 by Megan Hart
ISBN 1-59279-751-2
Cover Art © 2006 Trace Edward Zaber

Layout and Formatting provided by: ElementalAlchemy.com

PUBLISHED IN THE UNITED STATES OF AMERICA

*For the internet, iTunes, iPod and my iMac:
without you I'd be lost and despairing.*

*For my friends, in real life and online,
who keep me going.*

And for DPF, who keeps on keeping on...

TABLE OF CONTENTS

Amidst A Crowd Of Stars 1

Emerald Isle 39

Everything Counts 77

Moonlight Madness 109

Monster In The Closet 125

AMIDST A CROWD OF STARS

UNEXPECTED

AMIDST A CROWD OF STARS

Today

The medica was young, perhaps just out of the training academy. She still wore her uniform crisp and pressed, her blue hair slicked back from her forehead and held in place by the woven band marked with the symbols of her profession. She gave the man at the patient's bedside a warm grin and patted his shoulder.

"How nice of you to stay with your grandma all night."

The man was handsome enough to make her flutter her eyes. His dark hair, streaked by the harsh Lujawedan sun, fell to his shoulders in sheaves that made her fingers itch to run through it.

His hair might show the affects of the sun, but his face showed no sign of weathering. He smiled, his hand in the patient's, thumb stroking the paper-thin skin of her hand over and over.

"This is my wife," the man said without any condemnation at her assumption, for which the medica was grateful.

"Oh, I beg your pardon."

He looked back to the woman in the bed, her eyes closed and face pale. He leaned forward to stroke her hair, long and lush and bleached white the way the sun bleached everything on this planet. His hand caressed her cheek for a moment, and in the presence of such admiration, the medica blushed and left the room.

* * *

UNEXPECTED

Yesterday

Marrin woke to the feeling of kisses on her bare stomach. She kept her eyes closed, but smiled as her husband trailed his lips along her skin to the slope of her hip. She waited, breath held, for him to continue, and he didn't disappoint.

He never did.

"Good morning," he whispered against her skin, teeth nipping in a way that made her sigh. "The sun is shining again."

This made her laugh, as it always did, for on Lujawed, the sun almost always shone. "Good morning."

She cracked open an eye to look down at him settled between her thighs as though he had no place else to be for the rest of the day. He laid his cheek on her thigh and let his hand stroke along her side. Her hand came down to rest on his hair, the glorious length of it that time and the sun could burnish but not diminish.

"I love you, Keane." The words slipped out without effort. She stroked his hair, like silk against her fingers.

"I love you, Marrin." He turned his lips to kiss the skin beneath his cheek, then grinned. "I would love you better."

She parted her thighs in reply, her eyes already going half-lidded in anticipation of the pleasure he would bring her. She heard his chuckle and felt the hot puff of his breath on her clit a bare micron before his lips kissed her there. She sighed, shifting. His hands curved around her hips to hold her to him while he began to make love to her with his mouth.

He kissed and licked her gently no matter how much she squirmed, taking his time. He always did. It was one of his charms, this constant ability to give his full attention to any task he performed, as though he had all the time in the world to complete it.

Because he does, she thought, lifting her hips as his mouth teased her flesh. To a Seveeran whose lifespan was limited only by accident or choice, anything worth doing was worth taking time for.

Her breath caught as his tongue fluttered against her folds. He nuzzled her, then parted her with his fingers to taste her. His low noise of arousal urged her own, and she answered with a gasp.

"Keane!"

He didn't answer with words. He slid a finger inside her to stroke in time with his tongue. He'd found the pace she adored. Smooth, steady, alternating patterns of light tongue flicks and harder licks. He slid another finger inside her love-slick passage, filling her.

She wanted more, but he wouldn't give it, her deviously sensual husband. No. Keane teased her, adding a twist to his hand that had her crying aloud and clutching the bedclothes as her hips rocked upward. He pressed his mouth to her clit, not moving lips or teeth or tongue. Letting her get off by rubbing her clit against him. Letting her dictate the pace and pressure. Giving over to her control...until she was on the edge and ready to soar over. Then he pulled back, hand stilling, and blew repeated puffs of air against her pulsing clit and would not touch her with more than that no matter how she begged.

When she calmed, he withdrew his hand micron by terrible, exquisite micron, and slid up her body to kiss her mouth. His cock nudged her opening, and though she was so wet for him the sheets felt damp beneath her, he did not enter her.

"I love you," he murmured in her ear, sending shivers to perk her nipples into peaks as hard as lliwrock. "One hundred rotations I've loved you, Marrin, and I would have a thousand more."

She opened her eyes and linked her hands behind his neck to pull him back to her mouth. "I'd give them to you if I could."

He made no more talk but slipped inside her with the practiced ease of long experience. He paused when he'd filled her and she marveled anew at how well they fit together. Like pieces of a puzzle carved by Adonai's own hand. He moved, his face pressed to the curve of her shoulder. Slow, long strokes, his stomach pressing her clit with every movement until she was back on the edge again.

She clutched him, fingers drawing trails down his back to cup his muscled buttocks. She pulled him closer. They melded, joined, moved as one. He withdrew and slid in again, the tip of his cock extending to nudge the entrance to her womb. Out again and his penis contracted. In, and it lengthened.

The dual sensation of his external and internal stroking never failed to send her to heights of pleasure she'd have said were impossible if she hadn't lived with them for so long.

"I love the way you take all of me inside you." Keane moved faster. His hand found hers. Their fingers linked. He lifted his head to look into her eyes, and the love shining in his gaze lifted her up and up, all the way to the sky.

Her orgasm fluttered at first, then rippled and at last exploded through her. She gasped and cried his name, pleasure making her mindless for a moment. Her body tensed and relaxed.

He gasped and shuddered, his back arching as he thrust into her one last time. She loved seeing him this way, perfect features creased with ecstasy. His body slowly ceased to jerk and shiver, and he lay down on top of her to nuzzle against her neck.

"Good morning," she said after a moment. "It's always a good morning when you wake me like that."

He laughed, the sound rich as cream dribbled over fresh-picked berries. He got up on one elbow to look at her. "Are you sure I can't convince you to come with me today?"

"Not a chance, sport." She settled herself on the pillows as he shifted his weight off her. Now that the lovemaking was over, her hip had flared into the same dull ache that always plagued her. They didn't speak of it, but he knew and was careful of it.

"No?" He kissed her beneath her ear. "I've heard the silk merchants will be showing off their new fashions."

She laughed and pushed at his shoulder to let her up. "Where do I ever go that I'd need something like that?"

"It's not a question of need, but want."

She glanced over her shoulder at him still sprawled in their bed and looking so handsome it made her throat close with emotion. "You go and have a good time."

He stretched out. Still sinewy and firm, still looking as he had the day she'd met him in the starport. Nothing had changed about him. No wrinkles, no lines, no bulge or bumps of age.

And she...Marrin caught a glimpse of herself in the mirror over the dresser. When had she gotten so old?

She got out of bed, her throat still closed and her breath short. She went to the window and drew back the outer curtains, but left the inner set alone. They were sheer enough to let in the light but keep out the sun's harshest rays. In the daylight she could see every blotch and bump on her skin, every imperfection.

"Marrin?"

And then she turned from the sight of her own face, not needing to see anything but how she looked reflected in Keane's gaze. "Yes, sweetheart?"

"Are you all right?" He'd sat up and was looking concerned. "You look pale."

She nodded, her hand going to her throat to try and ease some of the pressure there. She tried to catch her breath, but could not. She tried to speak, but could say nothing. She reached for him, and his face was the last thing she saw as her knees crumpled and dropped her to the floor.

*　*　*

Forty rotations ago

"What will you do tomorrow?"

Marrin turned to look at her assistant. Former assistant, she corrected herself. As of this moment, Marrin Levy no longer had an assistant, or needed one. It had taken a full two rotations to get all the details sorted out, but now that everything had been taken care of, she was more than ready to let go.

"Sleep in for one." She smiled at Darlin. "Have a leisurely lunch in the courtyard. Perhaps go shopping in the afternoon for the girls' birthdays."

"Sounds perfect." Darlin's bright grin shone against the dark skin of his face. "I'm envious."

"You know you're always welcome to visit us."

He reached out to her for a hug. "We'll all miss you, Marrin."

"It's time for me to step down." She returned his hug without even a sentimental tear at the thought of leaving the position she'd had for the past eighty rotations. "Time for me to spend some time with my husband."

"Keane will keep you busy." Darlin laughed and squeezed her again.

"I'm sure he will."

And Keane, it seemed, intended to start keeping her busy the moment she returned home that evening. Marrin saw the glow as she walked up the curving stone path leading to the house she shared with Keane. She paused, looking over the low-slung white building nestled into the red Lujawedan earth. He'd lit candles in every window.

More candles illuminated the entryway and made a path through the smoothly curving halls toward their sleeping room. She followed the flickering light. By the time she got to the bedroom, her heart had already started to beat faster.

"Keane?"

More candles beckoned her toward the bath chamber. Smiling, she followed them and found her husband waiting for her. Glancing over his shoulder, he looked up as she entered, and she caught her breath as she did so often when he looked at him.

"You're late," he said gently, turning. The candle glow lit his bare skin with a loving touch, hiding scars and making shadows turn every glimpse into seductive temptation.

"They had a party for me," she explained. "I had to say goodbye to everyone."

He smiled and held out his hand. "Everyone will miss you."

She went to him and took it. "I'm ready to give it up. Ready to be home with you all day long."

He bent his head to brush his lips along hers. "I'm ready to have you here."

So many years, and still that simple first kiss upon meeting after being apart never failed to send a shiver of desire through her. Marrin tilted her head as Keane's hand cupped the back of her neck. His fingers massaged the two small spots at the base of her skull, eliciting an immediate response.

Her moan made him laugh. "You're still tensed up."

"Not so much, now." She pressed herself against him, and the heat of his skin seeped through her *nawe*.

The hand not on her neck slid to her hip and began inching the floor-length garment upward with his fingertips. Cooler air, blown through vents in the bath chamber floor, caressed her feet and ankles, then her thighs as he gathered the thin cloth and exposed her skin.

Keane kissed her, lips parted. She opened her mouth wider beneath his to let his tongue stroke her. His hand slipped around from her waist to cup her between the legs. The heel of his palm pressed her clit while he used his fingers to nudge aside the filmy barrier of her panties. He stroked along her folds.

"You're so wet for me."

"Always." The word came out low, throaty.

He pulled her closer, the hand on her neck sliding down to palm her buttocks and gather more of her *nawe*. In another few moments he'd pulled the garment up to her hips, then over her ribs and head. He tossed it to the floor.

"You won't need to wear that again." He bent back to kiss her again, both hands on her ass, holding her close to his already-hard penis.

She laughed. "No? I do if I intend to ever go anyplace other than this compound."

He nipped her jaw, urging her with his teeth and lips to tilt her head back so he could slide his tongue along her throat. "I intend to keep you here with me…naked."

"All the time?" Her giggle became a gasp as he bit the tender spot between her neck and shoulder. His hands rubbed her buttocks, dipping between her legs to brush her folds from behind before sliding up again along the ridge of her spine.

"All the time."

Marrin put her hands flat on his chest. His heart thumped under palm. She traced the indent running from his throat to the place his navel would have been had he been Earther like her. It was sensitive, that thin place in his skin where once he'd been connected to the artificial womb in which he'd been grown, and her touch made him shiver.

She didn't bother arguing with his impractical suggestion she never wear clothes again. At that moment, the thought appealed to her so greatly, she was more than willing to believe in it. She kissed his chest and tasted his warmth. Keane's arms closed around her, cradling her.

"I love you," she said, emotion all at once hitting her harder than she'd expected. "I would never have been what I am today if not for you."

He kissed the top of her head. "I love you too, Marrin."

His fingers traced lazy circles on her bare back. She looked to the sunken tub set into the tiled floor and smiled. He'd filled it with steaming water and floated gillyflower petals on top. She breathed their scent and tilted her head back again to look up at him.

"Are you going to join me in there?"

He smiled revealing bright, white and shining teeth. It was the happy grin that had been the first thing she'd noticed about him all those years ago.

She needed help getting into the steaming water, but Keane held both her elbow and her hip in such a way she was able to slide into the tub in what seemed an effortless motion. He knew how her hips and knees pained her. He was always there to lift and carry for her, to open doors, to help her with stairs. He never made it seem as though she couldn't do it on her own. Always, every assistance came as though it sprang naturally forth from everything else he did to care for her—everything he had done for years.

Marrin settled into the water with a sigh and breathed in the scent of the flowers. He'd added oil to the water, too, and it glided along her skin.

"Such luxury," she teased. "An entire tub full of water, just for me?"

"Maybe I'll have to share it."

"Maybe you will."

The water slopped over the sides of the tub when he got in, and they both laughed. She slid into his arms, her back against his front, and he cradled her.

"I can remember when there was no water for bathing like this. When we washed once a week and used the bathwater for irrigation."

"We still do," he reminded. "Only now it goes out through a drain and into the earth, instead of being poured by hand from the tub."

She laughed. Against her back, his cock lengthened and grew hard. Marrin nestled closer. Keane's hands came around to cup her breasts.

Her nipples tightened instantly beneath his skilled fingers. He pinched them lightly between his thumb and forefingers, tugging gently. Pull, release, and again, followed by a circling motion.

Her clit pulsed in time to his treatment of her nipples and she parted her legs. The hot, slick water washed over her pussy like a tongue, licking. Marrin shuddered and let out a small moan.

Keane slid one hand down her side, over her hip, then between her legs. His fingertip unerringly found her swelling bud. He stroked it, dipping low to caress her folds before moving back up to place a steady pressure on the bundle of nerves.

The fingers on her nipple pulled and released without ever letting go. In a moment, the fingers on her clit did the same. Pull, release in small, steady movements that nonetheless caused the sensation to build up and up until she became mindless with it.

She writhed, back arching, legs spreading to allow him free access to wherever he wished to touch her. "Keane—"

He murmured words of love in his native language she didn't need to understand to know their meaning. He lifted her in the water, the hand on her clit leaving for a moment to slide beneath her buttocks. His other hand came down to grip his penis and guide it inside her. He seated her on him, her head tilted back to rest upon his shoulder and her breasts pushed upward, out of the water.

He moved her, letting the water aid him. Keane thrust inside her with exquisite slowness. His fingers went back to circling on her clit.

The shallow thrusts rubbed her just behind her pubic bone and made her moan and shift, seeking to thrust herself further down on his shaft. Wanting to fill herself with him. His cry as she succeeded forced an answering one from her throat.

She rocked herself against him, losing herself in the pleasure washing over her. The slap of the water against her only aided the sensation of his hands on her. It rushed over her clit and breasts and belly, caressing her in every place his hands were not and in other places when his fingers found those.

His cock extended and contracted inside her as he neared his climax. Knowing he was so close made her orgasm tumble toward her like rocks rolling down a hill. A flurry and rumble of sensation built inside her, gathering together, gaining speed, centered in her clit, but drawing sensation from all the rest of her body.

He gave her what she wanted. Hard, solid thrusts deep inside her. Hard enough to lift her from the water. Marrin didn't care. She arched to create a better angle. Keane's lips found her temple. Her hand came around to run her fingers through his hair.

They both spoke but what words came out, Marrin could not have said. Words of pleasure, senseless. Lovetalk, Keane called it. An outpouring of emotion echoing the outpouring of sensation in their bodies.

Keane no longer rubbed her clitoris. He put his palm over it. His thrusts moved her against his hand, the stimulation more subtle, but no less perfect.

Marrin's orgasm rippled through her. Her fingers tightened in his hair. She cried out. Her tunnel clenched his cock, earning her a cry of pleasure from his lips.

It sent another wave of climax over her. She tensed, relaxed, tensed again when he thrust once more and held her hips hard enough to hurt if she hadn't been so filled with ecstasy.

"Marrin," he whispered.

The water ceased its sloshing and rippled gently. The scent of gillyflowers covered them. Marrin floated in her husband's arms, replete.

* * *

Forty-two rotations ago

"You're going to wear a hole in the floor."

Keane's calm bemusement was usually enough to diffuse her, but not this time. Marrin looked up at him but had to blink hard, twice, to get her eyes to focus on his familiar beauty. He reached out a hand, and she took it.

"She'll be fine," he told her. "She has the best medica. The best care. And she's stronger than you think, Marrin."

Marrin linked her fingers in his. "She's been in labor for more than a day. If she doesn't have the baby soon—"

"They will take care of her," he soothed. "And Sarn is with her. He will let us know when something happens."

Marrin nodded, knowing Keane was right. She gave him a grateful smile. "Now is the time when you remind me it's time for me to let go. Again."

He pulled her into his embrace with a gentle laugh and nuzzled her neck. "Aliya is with her husband, doing what mothers have done for hundreds of rotations. What you did, without benefit of such fine facilities, I might add. And you survived it."

Marrin looked around at the pale blue walls, the soothing art, the soft and comfortable furniture meant to cradle those waiting for news of their loved ones. "I gave birth to Hadassah in my own bed with the *vadid* howling in my ears and Raluti telling me the wind meant good fortune for births. What she really meant was it was fortunate for those outside the hut because they wouldn't have to listen to me screaming."

"But you did it," he reminded. "In a place you didn't know, with people who weren't yours."

She squeezed his hand. "So much has changed since then. There were no medicas. No town, really. No paved roads."

He nodded and smiled and hugged her closer against him. "Aliya will be fine. She'll have this baby in a few more hours, and you'll be a grandmother."

Marrin made a small groan. "I don't know if I'm ready to be a grandmother."

"Well, I'm ready to be a grandfather." Keane ran his hands down her back. "I look forward to cradling a small one."

Marrin tightened her arms around him. "Are you sorry you never had any of your own?"

"I have three of my own. Just because they didn't spring from my seed makes them no less mine."

She tilted her head to look at him. How lucky she had been the day he walked off the freighter with her letter in his hand.

"I love you."

He kissed her forehead. "I love you, too."

The hours passed. The baby was brought forth. The mother and father were congratulated and the infant admired, the family expanded by one.

UNEXPECTED

Marrin held her tiny newborn grandson in her arms and sought signs of Aliya's father Seth in the tiny boy's face. She found it in the crinkle of his forehead as he frowned, and she wept, kissing the spot and wetting his little face with her tears.

At home, when they had left the new parents to rest, Marrin stayed quiet. Thinking. Lujawed had rotated past its sun a hundred and twenty-five times since she'd arrived, a young woman with two small daughters and an idealistic, unrealistic husband set on changing their lives.

Their lives had changed all right. Seth had found the plot of land granted them by the Interstellar Homestead Act didn't quite live up to the photos in the brochure he'd shown her. If they wanted green grass and a tidy little cottage, they'd have to work on it. Work hard.

Lujawed in those days was habitable only by sweat and effort. By hauling water up from wells dug so deep they needed to be lined with lliwrock to keep them from collapsing. By erecting buildings that could stand up to the *vadid*, the ever-present desert wind that howled and bit and ground away at the surface of everything, leaving it pitted and scarred.

They'd had help from the natives, grateful to trade their labor for the luxuries brought in on the Homestead Freighters. Nomads, the Lujawedi had no use for permanent dwellings. They didn't understand the need for roads, for sanitation facilities, for hospitals. Goggles that kept the sand from their eyes and water pouches that kept their beverages cold were welcomed and coveted. So long as the Homesteaders kept to their own sections of the planet, the Lujawedi didn't care what the newcomers did with it.

And amazingly, Lujawed remained amicably split between its nomadic natives and the newcomers who'd come seeking a better life. Unlike many of the other homesteaded planets, Lujawed had been settled without war. Marrin could take pride in being one of the original colonists. Every rotation they honored her at a city council dinner—but it had been several rotations since she'd been asked to sit upon the council.

That was the way it went, she supposed, turning from the window where she'd been staring. Out with the old and in with the new. Only she didn't feel old, damn it. On a planet that rotated twice as fast around its central sun, her years were doubled, but not her lifespan. She was a grandmother who felt like she ought to still be that young mother digging in the sand.

It was largely in part to Keane, who aged so slowly he seemed not to. Now Marrin watched him at his meditation in front of the small burning candle. The scent of the powder he burned tickled her nose, and she sneezed. He opened his eyes with a smile, unfolded himself from the floor and came toward her with long strides.

"Time for bed," he said.

She leaned back against him, and his arms came around to hold her close. He put his cheek to hers as they both looked out the window to the land that seemed only yesterday to have been barren and brown and now shone with soft green grass and vibrant desert flowers.

"So much has changed." Marrin sighed. "Keane, where has the time gone?"

He turned her in the circle of his arms and kissed her forehead. "Time goes. It's what happens to it. What's wrong?"

She tilted her head back to look up at him. "Nothing's wrong. We have a grandson."

"We do." Keane smiled and brushed the hair from her forehead with his thumb, then let his hand come down to caress her cheek. "And look at all you've accomplished."

"All we've accomplished," she corrected. "I'd never have made this estate what it is today if not for your help. I'd never have been able to manage the irrigation systems that let us grow that first crop of *udeji* melons. And now look at us. Landowners. Largest supplier of fresh *udeji* melon in the entire colony."

He smiled again and kissed her, letting his lips linger on hers. "You should think about retiring, Marrin. You've worked hard. Take some time to enjoy your new grandson."

She laughed and squeezed his bum. "You just want me to sit around here with you, getting fat and lazy."

"I beg your pardon." Keane made a show of sounding affronted. "Lazy I'll give you, but am I fat?"

She ran her hands over his hips, then up his taut belly and firm chest to link her fingers behind his neck. "Most definitely not."

Keane reached down and swept her up into his arms. He walked her to the bed and laid her down, stretching out along her body. "Not too heavy for you?"

She laughed and pulled him down on top of her. "No. Never."

Then he began kissing her, and she didn't think about melons or the desert or anything else but his hands on her. He lifted the hem of her gown to her thighs, then higher to expose her belly. Keane kissed the scars there. Her badges of honor, he'd always called them, the signs of her pregnancies. They'd always made her feel self-conscious before him, but to Keane they represented something so miraculous and glorious he never failed to make her find them as beautiful as he did.

Seveerans didn't reproduce with their own bodies any longer. Science had replaced childbirth. Seveerans procreated solely via artificially inseminated and cultivated embryos in a *crèche* system. To Keane, the fact Marrin had carried her own children inside her body and given birth to them seemed like something out of a fairy tale.

He gave only a moment to her marks, though, instead moving lower across her belly to the area between her thighs. She sighed when his breath fluttered across her clitoris. She gasped when he used his tongue to stroke it. Marrin closed her eyes and leaned back into the pillows, giving herself up to him.

Keane slid his hands beneath her buttocks to hold her closer to him. His lips and tongue began a familiar pattern. He knew so well how to please her. He knew just where and how to touch her. How hard or soft, fast or slow, how she needed him.

It wasn't instinctive, but rather years of experience that had given him such talent. Experience and enthusiasm. But most of all, love. Love allowed him to find the right spots to send her soaring, let him discover new places to make her gasp his name and arch her back under his caress.

Keane slid a finger inside her, pressing upward while he pressed down on her clit with his tongue. The dual sensation was exquisite. She shivered. Bright sparks of pleasure radiated outward from her pussy, up her belly, spiking her nipples and parting her lips in a breathy sigh.

"I love when you make that noise." He paused in licking her to look up. "It makes me so hard."

She smiled down at him. "And I love it when you get hard."

His answering grin made her heart pound. He bent back to her clit, nuzzling it lightly before beginning to lick again. He had her on the edge in another minute, earning a moan of regret when he pulled away to tease her. Keane loved to tease her to the edge and hold her off, bringing her close and refusing her release until she exploded under a breath or a whisper.

Tonight, Marrin had no patience for that. Her body craved him. She twined her fingers in his hair and pulled upward. Keane followed willingly, kissing her. The taste of her arousal made another low moan leak out of her. He thrust his tongue inside her mouth, mimicking the way she wanted him to push his cock inside her.

"Make love to me," she whispered against his mouth, her fingers moving again and again through the dark silk length of his hair.

She didn't have to ask him twice. Keane slid inside her slickness without effort, all the way to the hilt. He filled her completely. He moved in slow, smooth strokes, angling his body in such a way that he rubbed her clit with his every thrust. It drove her half-crazy, the way he did it, the stimulation not direct enough to send her over the edge, but tantalizing enough to keep her hovering on the verge of orgasm.

He buried his face in the curve of her shoulder. His teeth stung her. The small pain was enough to jolt her entire body upward. He thrust harder. She wrapped her legs around the back of his thighs, pulling him closer while her hands made furrows in the smooth skin of his back.

His low cry sent another wave of ecstasy through her. Sweat slicked their bodies as they moved. Keane moved harder inside her, hard enough to move the bed against the wall, which made her smile and laugh a bit, breathless, even as she moaned in pre-orgasmic splendor.

If her sudden vocal appreciation of his skills surprised him, Keane didn't show it. He responded by moving faster. Harder. Marrin's orgasm began in a thunder of beating heart and shouts.

A second one followed on the edge of the first with no more than a heartbeat between them. Keane kissed her as his body shuddered in its own release. He collapsed against her, though even in his pleasure he remembered to hold himself up on his arms so he didn't crush her.

They breathed together. In. Out. Completely in time with each other. Then he propped himself up and looked into her face. He kissed her. "Will you at least think about staying home with me?"

The seriousness in his question surprised her into sitting up. "You mean it?"

Keane rolled onto his back, one lean arm behind his head to support it. "I do."

"Keane, my work—"

"Your daughters and their spouses have taken over the company. You have shareholders and a board and secretaries and volunteers." He looked up at her, his dark eyes shifting color as they did when emotion moved him. "You've worked hard to get where you are. But now, can't you consider taking a rest?"

"I've worked hard and you've been behind me every step of the way. You've worked as hard as I have. And you've always refused any sort of official position in the company."

He smiled. "Those who matter know my place at your side. Those who don't will always assume I'm just your Seveeran houseboy. Pretty to look at."

She reached to caress his face. "It's been a long time since anyone accused you of being that."

"What I'm saying is, Marrin, why not let it be true? Retire. Stay home with me every day. I'll be your houseboy and make it worth your while."

She laughed and leaned down to kiss him. "You're wooing me."

His grin remained as charming as it had always been. "I am."

"Stop working?" Marrin leaned back against the headboard, thinking. "I'm not sure I'd know what to do with myself all day."

"Lounge in the garden, breakfast on the terrace, make love in the afternoon."

"Be lazy is what you're asking me to do, Keane."

"Take your reward," he corrected gently. "And let go so your children can also have a chance to prove their value with hard work."

She sighed. "You want me to let go of something I've spent half my life working to build."

"And I want you to spend the other half enjoying the fruits of it." Keane linked his fingers through hers. "I want you to spend the time with me."

And that, she decided as she looked down upon him, was reason enough to do as he asked, for Keane had never asked her for anything before.

*   *   *

Fifty-two rotations ago

The door opened and Marrin looked up, her mouth full of pins. "Sarai, good, you're here."

Her middle daughter, the fairest one, closed the door behind her and set down the bouquet of *udeji* melon flowers Hadassah had insisted on carrying for her wedding.

"You look gorgeous, Dassah." Sarai gave her younger sister an admiring look. "Jaron will faint when he sees you."

"I hope not." Marrin slid another pin into Hadassah's trailing hem. "We don't need any fainting going on."

Hadassah took a deep, shaky breath. "Ma, do I look all right?"

Marrin stood and looked into her daughter's face. Her baby, the child she'd borne in the desert, the one of her daughters who'd known no other world than Lujawed.

"Gorgeous." She smoothed Hadassah's dark curls over her shoulder. Of the three girls, Hadassah looked the most like Seth, who had never even had the chance to see her. Marrin hugged Hadassah tight, not caring that she crumpled the gown of fine Lujawedi flaxene. "Absolutely beautiful."

The door opened again, this time for Aliya. "Are you ready?"

Hadassah lifted her chin and took a deep breath. "I'm ready."

Marrin looked at her children—the three bright, shining lights she had produced—and her throat closed with emotion. "Your father would be so proud."

Her girls hugged her then, and the four of them clung to each other in the circle they'd always made.

The door opened a third time, this time to Keane, who held back for a moment upon seeing the clustered femininity which had left him flustered and left out on occasion in the past. "We're ready whenever you are, Dassah."

Hadassah, who had never known another father, had nonetheless been the one who'd clashed most fiercely with Keane over the years. Marrin would walk Hadassah to the wedding canopy alone. Now Keane looked discomfited, and Marrin knew her husband well enough to know he didn't want to be accused of interfering.

"Keane..." Hadassah stepped free of her sisters' and mother's embrace. She reached for his hand and he took it with a look of surprise. Her voice clear and unclogged by tears, she said, "I know I've been an awful brat to you in the past. And I know you've always been patient with me, even when I didn't deserve it. I appreciate more than you can ever know how you agreed to my wishes about this wedding...but I've been stupid and stubborn, and I've changed my mind. I'd be honored if you'd walk with me to the canopy."

Marrin watched as his eyes changed from black to blue to green, expressing his shifting emotions.

He nodded and squeezed Hadassah's hand. "I'd be so honored to walk with you. If that's what you really want."

"You're the only father I've ever had." Hadassah's voice broke at last. "And I know I haven't often shown it, but I love you."

Then they all cried except for Keane, whose eyes didn't shed tears, and they hugged and kissed, and then it was time for Hadassah Levy to become Hadassah Levy Curani.

No bride had ever looked lovelier, no mother had beamed brighter with pride, and no father had ever given away a daughter so tenderly. It had been a perfect day, with food and family and friends. At the end of it, exhaustion claimed Marrin, and she tumbled onto her bed face down before rolling onto her back with a sigh. Keane laughed gently from the doorway.

"The last to go," he said, shedding his formal jacket. "And now, we're alone. The whole house to ourselves. We've never had that."

Marrin watched him undress, her eyes lingering on his body in constant appreciation. "Have you ever wished it had been different when you came? That we'd had the chance for a honeymoon like most married people get?"

He turned from the dresser where he'd been placing his watch and the interlocked chain he wore around his wrist. "Do I wish I'd been able to spend a week with you at an overpriced tourist resort indulging in decadent sex and overeating bad food? No, Marrin."

She laughed. "I mean do you wish we'd had the chance to be a couple before we were a family."

Again, he shook his head and stepped out of his trousers, hanging them with the same neat efficiency he always did. At last fully naked, he moved toward her and stretched out on the bed beside her.

"The moment I stepped off that freighter and saw those three little faces, I was in love," Keane said. "Falling in love with you came later and was a pleasant side benefit."

She nudged him with a frown, but his answer pleased her. "You don't think it would have been easier without the girls?"

"Easier? Undoubtedly." He put his hand flat on her belly, fingers splayed. "Would I wish it had happened differently? Never."

He leaned down to kiss her, his tongue urging her lips to open. His breath was sweet from ceremonial wine. She licked his lips, tasting.

"It would've been easier to make love to you at the beginning without three little ones always underfoot," he whispered as his hand began a lazy ascent toward her breasts. "But maybe we can make up for it now."

"Pretend this is the first time?" she teased.

"If you like." His hand cupped her breast.

Her nipple rose beneath his palm. Keane rubbed his thumb across it. The barrier of her dress blunted the sensation but made it no less delightful.

"I was so nervous that first time. I don't think I'd want to repeat that."

"You were nervous?" He laughed. "I was afraid I wouldn't please you and you'd send me back."

"Keane, you weren't!"

He paused in kissing her to look into her eyes. "I was."

She'd never known he'd been afraid, too, the first time they had made love. The admission touched her. She put her hand to his face.

"I couldn't have sent you back," she said. "I loved you too much to live without you."

His tender kiss hadn't changed in all the years they'd been together. Familiarity couldn't steal the sweetness of it, or quench the fire he always created when he put his mouth on hers. No matter how many times they joined, each time was as exciting and fresh as the first time.

"You're not naked," he whispered in her ear. "And I am."

She remedied that by sitting up and tugging her dress off over her head. "We can't have that."

His low chuckle parted her thighs. His hand stroked the curls there, finding the already upright button of her clit and pinching it lightly. He rolled it between his thumb and forefinger before moving his hand down lower to slide a finger through her folds.

Slickness, begun at the sight of him undressing, already coated her. He brought some of it up to coat her clit, making it slippery. He rubbed her in small, tight circles interspersed with an occasional up and down stroke that had her whimpering in short order.

He kissed her mouth, her cheek, her jaw, down to her collarbone where he nibbled along the ridge and smoothed his tongue across her skin. He moved lower to suckle her nipples, one then the other, while his hand continued to work between her legs. Marrin looked down to see him stroking himself, too, the thickness of his cock appearing and disappearing into his fist as he pumped it.

"Come here." She reached for him.

He shifted on the bed so she could reach his penis. He kissed her hipbone. She angled her head just a bit, and took him into her mouth.

His low, strangled moan sent a pulse of pleasure through her that she could so affect him. Marrin slid his cock down the back of her throat as far as she could until her lips touched his belly.

His hand stuttered in its movement against her clitoris as she sucked him harder. The break in his rhythm only gave her more pleasure, brought her closer to orgasm faster. Her clit throbbed and her hips moved as she slid her mouth up again, then down.

UNEXPECTED

"Marrin, I love it when you take me all the way in your mouth."

His throaty words made her body tingle. She loved that about him, his ability to tell her exactly how he was feeling at all times during their lovemaking. What he liked, what he wanted, how to please him.

Before Keane, Marrin had never spoken during sex. Orgasms were like buried treasure. "X" marks the spot. Find the map, follow clues, and maybe you'll hit the jackpot.

Keane had shown her the freedom of speech, of telling her partner exactly how she liked to be touched and where, exactly what would work to get her off.

"I want to be inside you," he murmured even as he pushed himself deeper into her mouth.

She gave him one final, loving suck and then let him go. She got onto her hands and knees to look down at him, his eyes gone yellow in his arousal. He licked his lips, and before she could move, Keane got behind her and slid inside.

A moan escaped her as he filled her. Her butt tipped upward as she put her forehead to the bed, her hands on either side of her head, bracing herself. In this position he could grip her hips to move her, use a hand to slide around in front and tweak her clit while he thrust. He could go deeper, harder, and she gasped out in pleasure as he did.

"You're so beautiful," he told her as his hands rubbed circles on her buttocks and the small dimples on either side of her lower spine. His fingers traced the jut of her shoulder blades, the line of her backbone, and the cleft of her ass. He thrust inside her slowly as his hands caressed her body.

Climax stole her words. She pushed herself backward against him, needing him to thrust harder. To fill her. He groaned. She answered. Their pace quickened.

His erection stretched her. She settled her legs wider, pushing upward on her elbows. Keane reached around to press his fingertips to her swollen clit, and Marrin cried out. She pushed herself harder against him, each movement dragging his fingers along her erect button and stabbing his cock into her core.

They moved together in perfect time. The dual sensations of his erection inside her and the pressure of his hand on her clitoris was enough, at last, to send her over the edge.

"I want to hear you come," he said. "Nobody will hear you but me."

He was right. They were alone. After all the years in a house filled with children, they were at last alone. She screamed out her ecstasy, voice hoarse and her breath leaving her in great gasps as her orgasm pounded through her. Nobody to hear them, not now. Not with the girls all grown with families of their own. The time of quiet, furtive lovemaking had passed. Now there was no need to be silent in their passion, and the thought of it made her open her mouth and cry out, simply because she could.

He thrust harder and she bent forward to open herself to him, to take him deeper. She cried out again, another burst of climax filling her. She tensed, relaxed and tensed again. Keane cupped his hand over her, easing off the direct pressure that made her body jerk in the aftermath of her climax.

His thrusts became ragged. He cried out as she had, a wordless sound of joy. His cock pulsed. His fingers tightened on her hip.

A third time her vagina contracted around him, a smaller and gentler orgasm that made her moan and push back against him hard as he thrust forward one last time and shivered in his climax.

He stayed inside her for another breath, another heartbeat, and as she felt him begin to soften, he pulled out of her and lay down on the bed, pulling her into his arms to spoon her as they both caught their breath.

"Who needs a honeymoon?" she said when she could speak again. "This is much better."

He kissed her between the shoulder blades. "It is."

And they slept.

* * *

Eighty rotations ago

Only ten rotations ago, there had been no school auditorium in which ceremonies like this could be held. Students had taken classes in a building much like the one room schoolhouses of their ancestral Earth. Like everything else in the colony, hard work had provided the new building with its bright, airy classrooms and the large auditorium in which they all now sat.

Sarai's class was the first to graduate from the new school. Marrin watched her middle daughter march down the aisle with the rest of her classmates, her fair hair bleached blonder now by the harsh sun that lightened everything over time. Today there were fifty students, an unbelievable number when she thought about the first few families had come to Lujawed. She'd never have imagined one day she'd sit in an air-cooled room and see her daughter receive a degree for an education as adequate as any she'd have received on Earth.

Seth had been the one to dream of this, the one to look beyond the barren desert and blinding sun to imagine green fields and a thriving town. This had been Seth's dream, not hers.

Keane's fingers linked through Marrin's and squeezed, and she gave him a grateful glance. Sarai's graduation had hit her harder than Aliya's, though she wasn't sure why. Maybe because her oldest daughter had always been the one to make the milestones and seeing Sarai make another only emphasized to Marrin how much time had passed in her own life. In another four years Hadassah would finish her primary education. By that time, the university would likely be finished, and she could attend an actual university instead of taking correspondence lessons.

Her babies weren't babies any longer, and though Marrin didn't want to hold them back, part of her mourned the loss of her role as young mother. They didn't need her any longer. Not like they had.

She half-listened to the speeches, her mind on the company she'd finally turned into a success. Ashco had turned its first profit this year. A year of good weather, and an unusually plentiful rain season had allowed her to siphon some of the expense she'd normally have spent on irrigation into finishing up the climate-controlled warehouses and implement the distribution system that allowed the crop to reach all parts of the colony before it spoiled.

Luck had been with them this year, no doubt about it. It meant money and security, and the realization of a dream and the success of the business contented her in ways she'd never expected. Marrin Levy, a businesswoman? She'd have laughed at the thought. Now, she couldn't imagine anything less.

Keane's arm rested along the back of her chair, and she stole a look him. Without him, she'd never have made it to this place. The fever that stole her first husband had left them bereft, alone in a harsh land that was not home. A young mother of two, with a third growing in her belly, struggling to plant and harvest a brown and bleached scrap of land without the man who'd brought them there...there had been so many times she'd come close to giving up. If she'd had the money she'd have taken her children and gone home, but he hadn't left them even with that.

Three years of struggle, of poverty, of hunger and back-breaking labor, had finally forced Marrin to send away for what the

Homesteaders called a "field-husband." A man to work her fields and help take care of things.

Love hadn't been meant to enter into it. She looked at Keane's face, his eyes trained on the stage where there were more speeches being made. His lovely, dear face, which hadn't changed since the day she'd first seen him.

He turned to look at her and they shared a secret smile. The speech makers stopped talking. The audience rose to clap and cheer for the graduates, and Marrin turned from the sight of her husband, the man who'd come to tend her fields, but who'd ended up tending her heart, and found Sarai's beaming smile.

The colony was still small enough to support group celebrations like this one. The tables had been set with flowers and pretty cloths. A band hired to provide music. Food, laid out in a bounty that proved to any who doubted how prosperous they'd all become.

Marrin watched Sarai chattering with her friends. Her other daughters Aliya and Hadassah had also abandoned the dull company of their parents to seek their companions. Marrin had a plate of salad and a glass of iced water, but wasn't doing much beyond looking around in amazed pride.

"You're Sarai's mother, aren't you?"

Marrin turned at the question to see a woman of about her own age she faintly recognized. "Yes. I'm Marrin Levy."

"Arlene Simpson. I'm Jack's mom."

Marrin didn't know Jack, but she smiled and nodded anyway. Keane came up beside her and put his arm around her shoulders, squeezing gently before stepping away to take the plate from her hands and begin finishing the salad.

"Hi," he greeted Arlene.

The other woman's eyes widened slightly. "Hello. I'm Jack's mom." Her smile thinned as she looked at Marrin.

Keane smiled and shrugged, more honest in his reply than Marrin had been. "Sorry, I don't know Jack."

"Jack Simpson?" Arlene's tone clearly said Keane ought to know him. "He might be a year or two behind you."

Keane paused with the fork halfway to his mouth, an eyebrow raised. "Sorry?"

Marrin tensed, her gut twisting. It wasn't the first time their apparent age difference had been brought up in casual conversation, but it had been quite a while. Anyone who knew them knew Keane wasn't as young as his Seveeran genetics made him appear.

"My son," Arlene said patiently, as though Keane were an idiot. "He graduated today with your girlfriend."

"My girlfriend?" Keane's face showed an amusement Marrin envied, but didn't feel. He looked around the room, clearly biting back a laugh.

"Well, yes...you're Sarai's boyfriend, aren't you? I just guessed you—"

"You guessed because I was here with Marrin and behaving in such a familiar manner that I must somehow be related to her, and you assumed for some reason I was here because of her daughter, who graduated today with your son." His smile remained pleasant, his voice light, but he'd set down his plate and put an arm around Marrin's shoulders.

Arlene looked confused, from Keane to Marrin and back again. "Well, yes."

"Marrin is my wife," said Keane without changing his tone.

If the woman's face could have blushed any more crimson, Marrin didn't see how. Arlene Simpson stammered and stuttered and backed away like Keane had somehow insulted her when really, she was the one who'd put her foot in her mouth.

It made Marrin feel no better to watch the other woman's distress. Much of the time she could forget her husband was of a different race that didn't age the same way Earthers did. She aged every day. Keane did not.

"Don't let her bother you," he murmured in her ear, his arm tightening around her waist which she was proud hadn't thickened in their years together. "She didn't know."

"I know."

Marrin put on a smile, talking with the rest of the parents and well-wishers, but by the time the day was over she had a pounding headache from gritting her jaw. Tears stung her eyes as she sought the privacy of her bath chamber and splashed cold water on her temples. Sarai had gone to a graduation celebration, taking her sisters with her, and the quiet house was a balm to her strained nerves.

The sound of a whistling teakettle caught her attention and she lifted her head. She was too far from the kitchen to smell the *udeji* blossom tea, but she knew that's what he'd be preparing. She went to the kitchen and found her husband. He'd set the table with her favorite mug, the teapot with steam curling from the ceramic top, and a plate of cookies. He'd included a vase with a flower plucked from Sarai's congratulations bouquet.

This simple act of caring moved her to tears. More emotion after a long, emotional day. The best part of it was she didn't need to explain herself to him. All she had to do was look into his eyes, and Keane knew just what to do to make it all better.

Or if not better, at least bearable. He took her in his arms and pressed his lips to her temple as he stroked her back. His fingers tangled in the hair falling over her shoulders—which she now noted with some distress was streaked even further with white. That the bleaching came from the sun and not just her age didn't help. They might all live on Lujawed, but most of them had come from Earth originally, and standards of beauty were the same.

"I thought it didn't bother me anymore."

His lips curved against her. "It shouldn't. It's only misconception."

"I know."

"I'm seven rotations older than you."

"I know that," she said, swatting him. "But you don't look it."

"And I never will," Keane said gently. "But that doesn't mean anything. Did you fall in love with me because of what I look like?"

"No," Marrin said, "but that you're gorgeous helped a lot."

He laughed and hugged her, rocking her in arms still strong from long hours working in the fields, though he no longer needed to labor that way. "I could say the same. The first time I laid my eyes on you, you took my breath away."

She scoffed. "I was covered in dust and had three screaming children circling me like satellites."

"A pearl covered in mud is still a pearl."

She tipped her head back to look up at him. "I love you."

"I love you, too."

His hands slid up and down her sides, resting at last on her hips. He shifted her around until she was snugged up against him. Heat flared in her belly at the feeling of his erection already straining the front of his loose trousers.

"We're alone," he reminded her. "The girls won't be home until tomorrow."

"However shall we occupy our time?"

Keane smiled. "I think I can imagine."

The kitchen table was just the right height for him to slide inside her while he stood between her legs while she sat on the table. The curved plazglass table warmed to her skin, bared in only moments when he lifted her skirt and tugged down her panties. One hand cupped the back of her neck and the other anchored her hip as he moved inside her. Marrin locked her ankles around his hips, pulling him closer, holding him tighter.

Sometimes they made love slowly, taking hours. Sometimes, like now, they came together hard and fast, with nothing more than a glance to serve as foreplay. It didn't matter. She was as ready for him now as if he'd spent half a day caressing her.

The teacups rattled in their saucers as his thrusts rocked the table, and Marrin let her head tip back, back, laughing and gasping her pleasure as he filled her.

"Touch yourself," Keane said, his voice hoarse. "I want you to come with me."

With Keane supporting her she had no need to hold herself up, and it was easy to slip a hand between them to stroke her clit in time to his thrusts. She cried out as she rolled the small button under her forefinger. Keane stretched and filled her, in and out, while she rubbed.

He kissed her, mouths open, tongues darting and becoming desperate as their mutual climax approached. Marrin heard a clatter and a crack but took no time to see if they'd at last made the cups fall over. She lost herself in her husband's kiss, in the pleasure of his magnificent, unique cock as it moved inside her, in the sensation of her own hand between her legs.

He gathered her closer, his grip tightening. Her face pressed against his chest. She found his skin with her teeth and tongue, tasted the salt and spice of his sweat and of their passion, and he groaned when she nipped him.

"Come with me, Marrin."

She already was. Bright sparks of joy filled her. Her body jerked. Keane thrust inside her, sending another burst of ecstasy exploding through her. She cried out, riding him, digging her nails into his shoulders hard enough to bruise him.

He thrust again, this time hard enough to move the table. His back arched. He shuddered, then relaxed against her, panting.

Marrin heard a slow dripping and turned her head to see they had, indeed, spilled the tea. It had made quite a mess on the floor, too, but at that moment, she couldn't rouse herself enough to care.

"You wear this old man out," Keane whispered into her ear, nuzzling and nipping before hugging her tightly.

"Never," she replied.

"You can try," came his teasing reply.

"I can try," Marrin agreed and put her arms around the man she loved.

*   *   *

Ninety-nine rotations ago

"Hurry, Keane! Hurry! It's starting!"

Aliya danced, holding her pot with both small hands. Sarai joined her sister, a mug in each of hers. The baby, Hadassah, no longer such a baby, but a girl of nine rotations, held a mixing bowl up toward the darkening sky.

Keane, his long, dark hair tied at the nape of his neck, stepped through the glass doors at the back of the house and onto the slate patio. He'd put on the shirt she'd made for him Marrin saw, and though she tried to pretend the sight didn't make her heart leap, it did.

"Keane, it's starting!"

"All right." He laughed and reached for the mug Sarai handed him. He tipped his face toward the sky. A drop of rain splatted him between the eyes and he laughed again, spreading out his arms as more water came from the clouds.

The girls squealed and held up their containers, trying to catch the still slow-falling raindrops. They danced in their festival dresses, their small faces bright with excitement. Marrin's heart hurt to look at their joy, so fierce and overwhelming was her love.

"Look, *Ima*, look! Flowers!"

And indeed, what had been moments before a brown and barren yard had now begun to bloom. More rain pattered down, soaking instantly into the parched ground. Green tendrils which had been dormant an entire season now sprang up from the ground so fast they could see them growing. Flowers, red, purple, white and yellow, bloomed on vines and stalks. The smell of them filled the air, and Marrin breathed deeply, astounded as always by the annual miracle.

The blessing of rain. Lujawed was a desert planet, its water held so deep within its embrace it took the deepest wells to reach it. Yet once a year, thankfully without fail, clouds gathered. The skies opened. And water, the gift without which they couldn't survive here, poured forth in torrents. Sometimes four days. Sometimes two weeks. Glorious, fresh, sweet and life-giving water.

UNEXPECTED

The Lujawedi called it *idvad*, and so the colonists had taken on the term, adopted the holiday festival when all work ceased and every attention was given to collecting and appreciating the sky's bounty.

Watching her daughters' dance, Marrin's throat closed with emotion. She held her face up to the sky, letting the rain hide the tears suddenly sliding down her cheeks. She blinked rapidly and her gaze fell on Keane, who looked up at her from where he bent, laughing, to help Aliya empty her pot of water into one of the rain barrels.

One full rotation had passed since the day she had gone to Bosie Starport to pick up the man who had answered her ad. One Lujawed rotation, one round of seasons, one passage of time, and yet so much more.

He stood, his dark eyes flaring briefly blue in the way he had that she'd found so disconcerting at first. Seveeran eyes changed color with emotion, unlike Earther eyes that always stayed the same. And now, not for the first time, Marrin wondered what other differences his race had from hers.

She blamed her shiver on the chill rain, but knew it had nothing to do with that and everything to do with this man she'd taken as her field-husband. Keane Delacore.

Though they wanted to, the children couldn't stay up all night. When true night fell, Marrin dried them off, dressed them in warm clothes and tucked them into beds to be soothed to sleep by the unfamiliar sound of rain pattering on the roof. They fell asleep in moments, and she took the time to touch their faces, each one so precious to her she could scarcely bear it.

Her girls, Earth-age nine, seven and four. Growing so fast and so beautiful. She tucked the blankets around them and left their room, closing the door behind her.

The rain had grown heavier. It slashed the windows and sliced at the grass that had grown up in the past few hours. Marrin slid the glass doors open and went outside, water soaking her instantly to the skin.

Baths were a luxury. She wanted to spend as much time as she could with water on her skin. She let it wash over her as she walked into the garden that hadn't been there earlier.

And he found him. Standing, arms outspread again, face tipped up to the downpour, eyes closed, mouth open to drink.

It seemed somehow too intimate to see him this way, in this ecstasy. She had shared a home with him for a rotation. Taken meals together. Argued and been kind, laughed and wept, labored with him side by side in the melon fields which were only now beginning to take full root.

She had spent a rotation with this man, who was no longer a stranger to her, but she had never seen him lose himself in such joy. She made to back away, to find her own place to stand and take in the rain, but Keane, at that moment, turned his head and saw her.

He turned slowly to face her, his arms going down. The shirt she had made for him of white flaxene and red embroidered flowers had gone sheer, showing every ridge and muscle of his chest. It made her knees feel as though they would not hold her; she stumbled at the sudden, unexpected sensuality of seeing Keane wet and outlined by red thread she had sewn with her own hands. She had seen him stripped bare to the waist many times, but this was somehow all at once more and too much.

She took a step back on the tiles made slick with rain. She stepped onto grass and soft earth, smelled the scent of flowers she crushed beneath her bare heel. Her hair clung to her as her gown did, molding itself to her body as his shirt hugged him, and she realized his eyes were roaming over her as hungrily as she was certain hers had over him.

She had seen his eyes go blue and green and only once, red with anger. Now they were tinged with amber and gold as he blinked. He'd taken away the tie in his hair and it fell over his shoulders and halfway down his back.

She took another step back. Keane moved fast, smooth, with agile grace she'd always admired. His hand caught her by the upper arms just as she teetered with uncertain steps on the mushy ground. She gasped at his touch, for other than an occasional brush of fingers when they passed each other something, Keane had touched her only once before.

He had never taken advantage of the rights granted a field-husband, never called on the contract they'd both signed which granted him conjugal rights in exchange for his labor. Keane had never pushed her, and she'd always been grateful…until now.

Now he slanted his head to hers without asking for permission. His kiss seared her, and Marrin opened her mouth to taste him. Her arms went around his neck. His went around her back, pulling her close. His tongue darted inside her mouth and she groaned.

She had almost forgotten desire. She had pushed it away for so long, since Seth's death from a native virus, that she'd been certain she'd never feel it again. Now it crashed over her, blooming inside her like the flowers had bloomed all around them, brought to life by the rain, and by Keane's hands on her.

He pulled at her dress, tugging it upward over her thighs. His hands trailed along her heated skin and she shuddered when his fingers reached the spot between her legs. He pressed against her and she cried out, the noise muffled inside his mouth, still kissing.

He lay her down on a bed of soft grasses and flowers and left her mouth to pull off his shirt. He took her hand and put it over his heart, which thumped so hard it moved her fingers against his skin.

"Do you want this?" he asked, voice hoarse. "Marrin, I have to know if you want this. If you want…me."

She nodded. "I want you, Keane."

Had he been afraid she would say no? He closed his eyes for a moment and his shoulders heaved, but when he opened his eyes again, he smiled. He stretched out along her to kiss her again. He put her hand on the bulge in his trousers and groaned when she curled her fingers around it.

Wet clothes were difficult to remove. They fumbled with desperate fingers, both laughing and kissing and shivering in the rain, but at last they were naked together and Marrin looked over his body in wonder. To see that his penis was basically the same shape and girth and functioned in the same manner was more of a relief, and she couldn't help reaching to touch him as he knelt next to her.

"You're perfect," she told him, cupping her fingers around his length. His erection throbbed at her touch, and she smiled. Not so different.

Her touch had made him shudder, but he still smiled. "Glad you think so."

"I wasn't sure—"

"You've heard stories?"

She nodded. Keane bent down to kiss her, his body covering and warming her. "Yes. It does extend and retract during lovemaking, but not enough to hurt you."

She let out a breathless giggle. "Good to know."

His hand smoothed away the hair from her forehead, then slid over her cheek, down her neck to her shoulder, further down to cup her breast. "You're sure you want this?"

To answer him, she brought him back to her mouth to kiss her again. He tasted so good, so sweet and fresh. It made her stomach leap and jump and her clit follow suit. He was smooth and firm and fully masculine. He was kind and a hard worker and good to her children.

She wanted him for all those reasons, but also for one more.

She loved him. The knowledge of it, of realizing what she must have known for months but ignored, made her gasp aloud. Her eyes opened and she stared into his.

"Marrin?"

She shook her head, not wanting to speak or ruin this moment they had taken so long to reach. Keane searched her gaze, but said no more. He bent back to kiss her throat. His mouth slid down as his hand had, and he suckled at her breasts one at a time until she gasped and put her hand on the back of his head.

His lips moved further down her ribs, to her belly, and she tensed. Hard exercise had kept her fit and poverty had kept her trim, but three children had changed her body in ways that would never recover. She bore scars. His lips traced them slowly, kissing each silver line as she tensed in mingled self-consciousness and desire.

"I've never seen such beauty," he murmured. "My people have nothing like this. No birth. You've done such a blessed thing, Marrin."

She had no time to reply because he had slipped lower. He parted her thighs and nuzzled her. She cried out, wordless, and put her hand over her face. Her pelvis bumped up against his mouth and he put his hands on her to hold her still. Her reaction should have embarrassed her, the enthusiasm of it made her blush, but it felt too damn good. His tongue found her clit and he licked her while she wiggled.

Whatever difference their races had, Keane knew how to make love to her. He used his mouth to bring her to the edge, then moved aside. He slid a hand under her buttocks and tilted her toward the sky. He parted her folds, exposed her to the beating spatter of the rain.

She'd gone mindless with pleasure. His tongue had made her throb, but this, this was unbelievable and unbearable. The rain, so rare and precious, pattered against her swollen flesh. Marrin broke, shattered, and exploded into shards of bright, shining desire.

He slid inside her while she was still pulsing. She climaxed again at once from the feeling of his cock inside her. She had gone so long without love, without touch. Now, as the skies had opened up, so did her body open to Keane.

He moved inside her, his face buried against her neck. Marrin put her arms around him, her fingers sliding along his wet skin to clutch his buttocks and urge him to move.

She didn't think herself capable of another orgasm. The two she'd already experienced had left her wrung and drained. She would concentrate on Keane's pleasure now, but to her surprise, her body began to respond again as he made love to her.

He pushed inside her, pelvis to pelvis, but then to her astonishment, his cock kept moving inside her. It grew. It nudged her cervix, which should have been painful but wasn't. When he pulled out, she lost the sensation of anything different. In again, and the feeling his penis moving deeper into her made her tunnel spasm around him.

He groaned. "Oh, you feel so good."

He moved faster, riding her. The ground had churned to mud beneath them. Slippery grass allowed their bodies to slide with every thrust. Desire puddled between her legs and in the pit of her belly again.

He moved faster, panting. She joined him. He gave a low cry and so did she. They moved in unison, giving and taking, each move as orchestrated as a dance they'd practiced for hours instead of performing for the first time.

He lifted himself onto his hands to thrust harder inside her, and to look down into her face. His eyes met hers. His face contorted as his climax approached. The sight of him in such bliss made her own fill her again.

She climaxed a third time, a small fluttering that didn't match the intensity of the first two, but was still enough to make her gasp aloud. Keane smiled when she did, eyes showing pleased surprise. In the next moment, they closed and his face contorted again.

He thrust inside her again, hard. His body tensed and he shuddered. Then he collapsed on top of her.

Marrin put her arms around him, holding him tight to her. Warmth filled her. She started to cry.

Keane got up on one arm to look at her. His body shielded her face from the rain. Concern filled his eyes. "Marrin?"

She shook her head, her emotion making her feel foolish and awkward in a way their lovemaking had not. Keane caressed her cheek. He smiled and bent to kiss her.

"I love you, too," he said into her ear.

And there in the garden, in the mud and rain with the smell of flowers blooming and going to rot, Marrin kissed the man who was no longer her field-husband, but her husband entirely.

*   *   *

One hundred rotations ago

Where was he? Marrin kept a firm grip on Hadassah's hand, no matter how hard the little girl tried to get away. Sarai and Aliya were running in circles around her, trying her already-thin patience. Marrin searched the crowd exiting the skyport, many of them greeting colonists who'd come out to meet them. Some carried the bags and bore the pale skin of new colonists as yet unburned by the harsh Lujawed sun.

She didn't see the man she sought any place. Tall, he had written. Dark hair to his shoulders. He'd be wearing a blue jumpsuit with white piping, and carrying a black leather bag.

His name was Keane Delacore. He was forty Earth years old, though Seveerans aged differently than Earthers and she shouldn't be surprised if he looked younger. He looked forward to meeting her in person, and her daughters.

If he didn't show up, she'd take her children and go back to the homestead. She would feed them and put them to bed, and maybe she'd go decadent and fill the washtub for a bath. If he didn't show up, she'd be no worse off than she already was—and maybe she'd be better.

If he didn't show up, she would somehow find a way to pay a labor crew to help her in the fields. How, she didn't know. She had no cash and, as yet, no crop to count on. She had nothing to barter, nothing to sell.

Seth had left her with nothing but three children and debt. In the three years since his death, Marrin had watched everything they had brought with them from home be sold off or break down in the harsh desert atmosphere.

He had been a good man with a wonderful dream, and it had not been his fault the immunizations against native viruses hadn't worked for him. It happened in .0001 percent of the population, a risk so miniscule even Seth, who calculated everything, had been willing to risk it. It wasn't his fault the *idvad* had been scarcer than usual their first two years on Lujawed. And it wasn't his fault he'd taken sick as their first crops failed, or when he died, but though none of those things were Seth's fault, there were days, many of them, when Marrin blamed her husband bitterly for her current situation.

The crowd of exiting passengers had trickled to nothing. Marrin kept her back straight, her eyes dry, her grip firm on Hadassah's straining hand. He wasn't coming.

"Come on, girls," she said at last, when the only person remaining in the starport station was the elderly Lujawedi sweeping the floors. "Let's go home."

As she turned, one last figure appeared in the skyport doors. A tall man with dark hair to his shoulders, wearing a blue jumpsuit with white piping.

He stepped cautiously through the doors and looked around. His eyes fell on their little group and he smiled, stepping forward, the look on his face one of a man greeting long-lost friends. He looked overjoyed to see them, and Marrin stepped back at the sight of Keane Delacore's smile. He didn't look forty. He looked even younger than her twenty-six years.

"Marrin Levy, I greet you," he said.

The formality of his speech took her aback for a second, but then she nodded. He spoke in Universal, in which she was competent, but not fluent. Perhaps he wasn't either.

"Welcome to Lujawed." Her voice sounded strained and brisk even to herself. She cleared her throat and held out the hand not holding Hadassah's. The little girl had shrunk behind her mother, watching from around Marrin's hip. "You must be Keane."

"I answer to that, yes."

He had an easy grin that tried to make her mouth twitch upward in response, but it had been so long since Marrin had smiled, the effort failed. His faded a bit when she nodded at him instead. He turned his attention to Sarai and Aliya, who had ceased their running and now stared with wide eyes at the stranger their mother had agreed to bring home with them.

"You must be Aliya." Keane pulled something from his pocket and held it out to the oldest girl, who reached out a trusting hand.

Instinct almost made Marrin intercept, but she resisted. This man had passed every test the Association for Interplanetary Spousal Provision had given him. He'd scored higher in morality, work ethic and intelligence than the other ten applicants Marrin's own analysis had matched her with. She was already technically married to him, and had been since the moment she'd signed the plazscreen at the agency office three months ago. So she stayed her hand and waited to see what he had brought.

"Thank you!" Aliya looked stunned and happy. She took the chocolate—a full bar, still sealed, and held it to her chest. "Oh, thank you!"

"And Sarai," said Keane, pulling another bar from his pocket. He had to bend further for her, but she took the present with no less enthusiasm than had her older sister.

"Thank you!" the girl cried and added a spontaneous hug. Sarai had always been the most affectionate one.

Keane's eyes met Marrin's over the top of Sarai's head. He looked away in a moment and focused on Hadassah, still clinging to Marrin's leg, though the bounty of chocolate had drawn her out.

"And Hadassah." Keane straightened, hand pulling out a third chocolate bar and handing it toward her.

Hadassah grabbed it and kicked Keane solidly in the shin.

"Hadassah!" Marrin's shocked cry echoed throughout the empty starport. "Oh, I'm so sorry—"

Keane shook his head, standing upright and giving a far kindlier smile to Hadassah than Marrin would have. "It's all right."

She cleared her throat uncomfortably. "She's usually not—"

"Marrin." Keane shook his head. "It's fine. Really."

Marrin nodded. "Shall we go?"

"Lead the way." Keane lifted his bag. "They told me the rest would be shipped out to your place once it goes through decontamination."

"Yes. I've brought the truck. It's outside."

The colony of Bosie couldn't be called thriving, but it had grown quite a bit since she and Seth had arrived six rotations before. Seeing it now and imagining what it must look like through Keane's eyes, pride and dismay warred inside her. To an outsider it didn't look like much, but to one of the original hundred and forty colonists, it was a metropolis built of love and sweat.

"You're seeing it at a great time," she told him as she hefted the too-big-to-be-carried Hadassah onto her hip and walked toward the truck. "Just after the *idvad*, when everything's in bloom. In a month, this will all be gone."

She indicated the flowers on vines covering most of the buildings.

Keane nodded. "I've read everything I could find about Lujawed. The holos are amazing, but not even close to seeing it for real."

That earned him a smile. She settled the girls into their seats and harnesses, then climbed behind the wheel as Keane took the passenger seat.

"It makes it all worthwhile," she admitted. "Knowing that for a few weeks out of the year, it's all beautiful."

By the time they got from town to the ranch, Keane had fascinated two of her daughters with tales of his journey.

Hadassah had always been the most stubborn one, the most spoiled and petted and cosseted, having essentially three mothers instead of only one. She glared at Keane the whole way home. She slammed the door in his face when they got to the house, and she stuck her tongue out him.

Marrin sent her to her room for that last insult and apologized once more to Keane, who smiled and shrugged, holding out his hands.

"It takes time," was all he said. "For everyone."

That first night, she offered him the choice of sides of the bed and lay stiff as iron when he climbed in beside her. Their contract stated there would conjugal benefits included in exchange for his work. Seth was the last man who had touched her. Aside from her children, he was the last person to have touched her in any other than the most casual ways.

She waited, eyes wide in the darkness, for the slide of a hand along her skin, for a mouth to seek hers. She listened for a shift in his breathing, for the rustle of clothes.

"I'm sorry," Keane said at last, his voice a richness dissolving into the darkness like honey dripped into tea. "I'm really tired from the journey. Would you mind if I just went to sleep?"

"No, of course not. Not at all."

And so he went to sleep, while she lay beside him for a long time, unable to sleep.

He worked hard by her side, and cheerfully, doing whatever task she set for him. He was vocal in his appreciation of her skills in the field, and of the meals she cooked, and of the way she washed his clothes. He never failed to thank her no matter what she did for him.

He won over Sarai and Aliya with his gentle manner, and he tolerated Hadassah's constant sassiness with patience and bemusement. Day after day he made himself a part of their family. Night after night he slept beside her in their bed, and night after night he made no move to make love to her.

"Good night, Marrin," he always said, and her answer returned, "Good night, Keane."

Months passed and she found herself laughing with him over after-dinner coffee, and discussing the girls' schooling, the crop, the repairs they needed to make to the house, and the sad state of their now-mutual bank account. She found herself remembering how he liked his breakfast prepared and making sure his clothes were mended and clean. She discovered herself staring at his hair as it fell over his broad shoulders and down his muscled back, now tanned by the sun.

She watched him when she thought he wasn't watching her.

When he'd said Seveerans aged differently than Earthers, he had meant their lifespans were longer. Once they reached maturity, they did not appear to age. They'd removed themselves almost entirely from the birth process. Genetics and specialized breeding had found a way to stop aging but not death; there was no fading away as there was in Earthers, no gradual decay and decline in quality of life as joints began to ache and vision faded, or memories began to disintegrate. If accident didn't claim their lives, Seveerans simply reached a time when they no longer wished to live, and then they no longer did.

It bothered her that he looked younger. When they went into Bosie, the people who saw them assumed Marrin Levy's field-husband was good for more than planting and harvesting. That she'd hired herself a young lover as well as a laborer.

Why it should bother her so much she couldn't say, since essentially, for all intents and purposes, that was what she had done. Bought a man to replace the one who'd died. What nobody else knew was that she and Keane weren't lovers. More like partners. And it wasn't any of anyone's business, was it?

"I think I'll go into town today," she said one morning.

Keane looked up from his newsform. "I'll go with you."

"No need."

He smiled easily. "I'd like to."

"I think I'd rather go by myself." Her words sounded stiff without reason, angry without reason, and she saw confusion in his eyes. She lifted her chin.

How could she explain that she didn't want to walk down the street and listen to the whispers that followed them? Especially when they weren't true.

He got up from the table. "Marrin, did I do something wrong?"

"No, of course not."

He frowned, an expression that rarely crossed his face, and moved closer. "You look angry."

"Well, I'm not, okay?"

Fuming, she crossed to the sink and ran the water, hard, though it wasted it. She splashed the dishes and slapped them with the sponge until he came over and twisted the faucet closed. He looked at her. "Tell me what's wrong."

"I just want to spend some time by myself," she snapped. "Is that so much to ask? Do we have to spend every moment together? Can't I just have some time to myself for once?"

She couldn't look at him. Shame turned her face away so she wouldn't have to see his look of hurt. She wiped her hands and started to move away.

He reached out and grabbed her upper arm. It was the first time he'd ever touched her deliberately. His grip was strong. It would leave bruises if she tried to yank her arm from his fingers. She didn't try.

"If I've done something—"

"You haven't."

"Marrin." Keane's gentle voice made her want to cry. "Look at me."

She did then because she couldn't help it. She kept her expression neutral. "What?"

"Are you going to send me back? Release me from our contract?"

His question surprised her. "No."

He nodded. "Good. Because I don't want to go back."

He released her and she stepped away. "Why not?"

She'd never asked him his reasons for agreeing to become a field-husband, for traveling light years from home to scratch out an existence on a planet as despairing as Lujawed. He'd never offered an explanation. She knew he wasn't a criminal because the agency had done a thorough background check. But beyond that, he'd never spoken of home or family.

She assumed his answer had something to do with some trauma on Seveer. A falling out with his family maybe. Or debts he couldn't pay. What other reason could he have had for coming here, and not wanting to go back?

He didn't answer her question, but posed another one of his own. "Do you wish you'd never sent for me? Or that I was someone different?"

"Yes," she said, though she didn't know why.

She turned her back and left the kitchen and Keane, and she went to town alone where she spent the day looking in shop windows at items she didn't need and still could not afford.

When she got home, she found the house quiet. The girls slept in their room and Keane in a chair by the window, a newsform on his lap. A covered plate in the coolbox made tears spring to her eyes again. She crept from the kitchen to stand in the living room doorway, watching him.

Then she went to his chair and stood. He opened his eyes.

"Because I'd miss you and the girls," he whispered in answer to her earlier question.

"We'd miss you, too," Marrin whispered back. "Come to bed."

She went to the bedroom and got into bed, and Keane got in beside her. They lay in silence for a few minutes.

"I'm sorry I'm not what you expected me to be," he said at last.

"I'm sorry I expected something different."

She heard him shift, felt the bed dip as he turned toward her. She waited for him to touch her, but all he said was, "Good night, Marrin."

"Good night, Keane."

* * *

Today

"Good morning, sir!" the medica chirped as she opened the blinds to let in the sun.

The poor man had fallen asleep by his wife's bedside, holding her hand. The medica smiled and moved closer to put her hand on his shoulder. She drew it back immediately with a small cry of surprise.

"Oh, my," she said as she ran for someone to come and help her.

Another medica joined her a moment later. "What's wrong, Pimmie?"

She gestured. "They're gone."

"Both of them?"

She nodded. "Yes. She was ailing, but the young man seemed fine yesterday."

The other medica moved closer. "She was his grandma?"

Pimmie shook her head, remembering the conversation of the day before. "Oh, no. She was his wife."

The other medica looked more closely at the man's face. "But he's Seveeran. They don't just die. They have to choose—"

"And he chose," said Pimmie, tears sliding down her cheeks. "He chose to go. When she did."

She smiled through the tears. "He didn't want to be without her."

"Well, now they're both in the stars," said the other medica. "Together."

And as she turned to leave the room, Pimmie though she heard a whisper, but when she turned back to listen, it had gone.

Good night, Marrin.
Good night, Keane. I love you.
I love you, too.

UNEXPECTED

EMERALD ISLE

UNEXPECTED

UNEXPECTED

EMERALD ISLE

"Surrender the emerald, *leannán*," purred the husky female voice in Eleanor's ear. "And I won't serve your lover to the sharks."

Eleanor looked to the edge of the plank, where Robin stood, trussed and blindfolded. Even his legs had been tied so tightly he could barely shuffle.

"*Póg mo thóin!*" Eleanor spat the only Gaelic she knew in the other woman's face. "Kiss my ass."

"Very well," her rival replied with a casual shrug. "Say goodbye."

"Robin!"

Eleanor woke, screaming, as she'd done for the past three nights. The bedclothes had tangled around her ankles. Her night rail clung to her body with sweat, and her hair had come loose from its braid. Untidy curls feathered across her cheeks, and she pushed them away impatiently as she fought to free herself from the blanket's grip.

"What is it, love?" Robin's voice curled around her in the darkness, and in the next moment, so did his hands. He gently extricated her from the tangled covers and pulled her back against him, spooning her. "Another nightmare?"

She nodded, though he couldn't see her in the dark. "The same one."

He chuckled. "She fed me to the sharks again?"

"'Tis not funny." Eleanor turned in the circle of his arms to press her face against his chest. "I didn't give her the emerald, and she killed you."

"But you did give her the emerald, love. And she didn't kill me." His lips brushed her forehead and he smoothed his hands down her back to cup her rear through the thin material of her night rail. He snugged her closer to him with both hands on her buttocks. "Don't worry about it, *mo chroí*, my heart. We'll find it—and her—and we'll get it back."

The tension coiled in her body as a result of the dream began to leach away under his touch. "She put her hands on you. I didn't like that."

He chuckled again, low in his throat. The sound reverberated in his chest, against her cheek. "She brought me no harm, love."

Eleanor frowned. "'Twas not harm she wished to give you."

Even now, the memory of that...that...Amazon touching Robin made Eleanor grit her teeth. "Grace O'Malley is a posturing, mannish hoyden!"

His fingers had been inching up her night rail while she spoke, and when his bare flesh touched hers, she sighed. He palmed her rear, his rough palms pleasantly scratching her soft skin.

"Gráinne Ni Mhaille is a well-respected pirate," Robin murmured as he worked his magic with his hands. "Her name is renowned."

"She's a vicious, greedy bint," said Eleanor, slipping her hands around his neck to pull herself up toward his lips. "She's got no right to our treasure."

His lips brushed hers. "She claims a portion of all commerce in these parts. 'Tis part of the code, love."

She parted her lips to allow his tongue to dip inside while she slipped a knee between his legs. "She didn't take only part, she took the whole damn thing!"

"To be fair, love, she didn't know the emerald was magic."

The tips of his fingers tickled between her thighs, brushing the edges of her nether curls. She nudged her knee higher, opening herself to his touch. Her nipples peaked and liquid heat pooled in her cunny. Her clit rubbed against his bare stomach, for Robin slept without clothes.

"Why do you keep trying to defend her?" she demanded. "She stole from you! More than just that emerald, which, I might remind you, we carried with us halfway 'round the world. That emerald was—"

"Going to lead us to the leprechaun's treasure. Yes, love. I know." His mouth possessed hers again, his tongue stroking hers. He curled his fingers more, brushing her curls again and finding her heat. He rocked her with infinitesimal movements against his belly, the firm muscles and crisp, curling hair teasing her clit into full erection. "Forget about that for the moment, *mo chroí*. I have another treasure I wish to find."

"Do you?" She smiled as his lips ran over her cheek and along her jaw, then down the slope of her neck to pause at the base of her throat.

He nipped and nibbled her there, as she gasped and arched against him. The slickness of her juices let her slide against him, creating a delicious push-pull of friction that made her thighs quiver.

Robin pushed her gently back against the pillows as he worked the buttons of her night dress. His fingers nimbly unhooked each one without hesitation, opening the material until she lay bare beneath him. His mouth traced the path of the opening buttons, down the slope of her breasts. He took one nipple between his lips and suckled it until she moaned aloud, then moved to the other. He flicked the taut bud gently with his tongue before taking it between his lips.

Her head tossed on the pillow and she was lost in the sensations. "Robin…"

He left a trail of wet heat by sliding his tongue down her belly. He tickled her navel, making her wiggle. Then he slid down further to find the upright nub of her clit. He kissed it. She jumped with a moan. He licked it. She writhed. He laughed, and the puff of his breath on her flesh made her sigh again.

"God's teeth, Nora, I love it when you make that noise."

She made it again, and this time it trailed into a whimper when he bent to stroke her smoothly with his tongue. Long, flat licks interspersed with small, circling flutters soon had her heart pounding so hard bright lights flashed in front of her eyes.

She lifted her hips to meet his mouth, rocking in rhythm with every touch of his lips and tongue. He slid a finger inside her, then another, and she cried out.

"I want to feel you around my cock," he murmured, every word causing his lips to brush teasingly on her clit.

Her orgasm surged within her like the sea readying itself for a storm. She crested and rode the waves of pleasure, then rose again, yet higher…higher…

"Break for me, love," Robin whispered.

She did, plummeting and rising again so swiftly she was left breathless. Her body tensed and released, her cunny spasmed, and her back arched against the bed. She cried his name followed by a wordless murmur of ecstasy.

In the next moment she felt his body on hers, and then his penis stretched and filled her. He moved steadily, his pace like waves licking the shore, advancing and retreating.

Eleanor hooked her legs around him and ran her nails down his back to rest at last upon the muscular cheeks of his ass. She caressed the warm flesh, urging him into her.

He buried his cock inside her willing tunnel, then withdrew and slid inside again to the hilt. His rear flexed and released under her hands. She lifted her hips to meet his thrusts, whispering his name and being rewarded with an answering groan.

He shifted himself a bit higher to press his pubic bone against the direct source of her pleasure. The steady, gentle pressure the position granted with each thrust meant she sailed toward another climax, smaller but no less exquisite than the first.

"Meet me there," Robin whispered against her lips.

"I'm there," she replied with a smile that became a gasp as her climax filled her.

He thrust again, his body shuddering, and groaned long and low. Her cunny's clenching masked the throb of his cock, but she knew he'd reached his release well, and knowing he'd spent himself inside her sent a few final flutters of pleasure through her.

He kissed her forehead, then her mouth, still seated firmly inside her. "The only treasure I truly need is betwixt your thighs, wife."

She laughed. "Ah, husband, love might make the world turn. 'Tis coin that fills our bellies. Surely you'd not wish me to go hungry?"

He growled, nipping her lips, then rolled off her. "No. I know how unbearably grouchy you get when you're not fed properly."

She dug her knuckles into his side. "Hush your tongue."

"Don't fret, Nora. We'll get the emerald back. And find the treasure. And give up pirating life for one on shore. An honest living, love. You and me and all the wee ones."

Emotion thickened her voice. "I truly don't need gold and jewels to make me happy, Robin. Being with you is enough to bring me joy for the rest of my days."

His arms slipped around her and pulled her close. "You'll have both, love. Me and the treasure. I vow it."

And she believed him…because he'd never lied to her.

* * *

I love the sea breeze in my face, Robin thought as the chill, salt-laden air lashed his long braids. The ocean was lover, friend, mother, child all wrapped up together. Its majesty and beauty never failed to move him; its fury never ceased to awe and amaze him. He'd never wanted anything more than life on the sea, with a ship beneath his feet and adventure ripe for the plucking.

Things had changed. He shaded his eyes and moved closer to the cliff edge, searching the ocean below for the ship he knew had to be cutting the waters. Now he had a wife. He never wanted to live away from the sea, but he no longer wanted to ride it to steal from others.

His Nora had adapted wonderfully to life as the wife of a pirate captain. She didn't get seasick and never complained about the lack of variety in their rations. The crew had loved her and accorded her a respect bordering on worship, for though his Nora had been born and bred a lady, she'd taken up the handling of all the crew's necessities without argument. She repaired garments, seasoned the food, made sure every man had his share of rest and sustenance. Her lilting songs lifted every heart, and though Robin had known many sailors who believed there could be only bad luck for ship with a woman aboard, none of his crew had harbored such superstition.

Except one. Barnabus, the betrayer. He'd sold them out for no more than the price of a flask of whiskey and an undiscerning whore's company. He'd shared the story of the leprechaun's emerald with a sailor enlisted by another pirate's crew, telling the other man how the jewel was fabulous enough to set up an entire crew for a lifetime.

The other man had told his captain. Gráinne Ni Mhaille, or as the English called her, Grace O'Malley. A fearsome wench who ruled the sea around Clew Bay, she'd done what any pirate would have done. She'd set out to steal the emerald.

Robin didn't blame her. He'd have done the same. Had done, in fact, though never to the pirate queen herself. And if it had been merely a jewel, he'd have let it go.

'Twas no mere jewel. It was a leprechaun's jewel, tied to the promise of wealth beyond imagination. He'd found the little green bastard in the Caribbean and stolen the first treasure marker, a coin that had led him to an island. He'd lost the gold, but come home with a better treasure in the end—his wife.

Unfortunately, Gráinne hadn't been satisfied with only taking the emerald. She'd also captured and conscripted his ship and crew. She'd shown Robin and Nora some mercy, at least, out of respect for a fellow captain, but she wanted to take no chances of easy retaliation. She'd put

Robin and Nora ashore in Galway with enough coin to buy them a week's lodging and food.

He could still hear the wench's laughter as she strode away, calling over her shoulder, "They might say many things about the pirate queen, but never let them say she is without mercy!"

It's that mercy that'll be her downfall, at least in this case, he thought, still watching the waves below. The sheer face of the Cliffs of Moher would give a man little enough purchase to climb, but he was fair certain that somewhere on their rocky sides was the entrance to the trove.

He'd tracked sightings of Gráinne and her crew for weeks, noting stories of any aberration in her routine. When she'd been spotted along the coast of the Aran Islands and then to the coast of West Clare just a few days later, he could think of only one explanation for the sudden change of course.

"My bloody emerald," he said aloud, still watching.

Wit and thriftiness had allowed him and Nora to travel here and secure lodgings. It pained him to see her working when she'd been meant for looking lovely, but she insisted she didn't care. Wiping tables and tending the fire at the inn earned them a free room, while his help in the stables gave them food…and time to scout the cliffs for signs of Gráinne and her ship.

And there it was. One of her many swift galleys, scourges of the Irish Coast. He watched this one cut through the water like a hot knife through butter. The rocky, narrow shore at the bottom of the Cliffs of Moher didn't have much on it. So when he saw Gráinne throwing anchor just off shore, he knew he'd discovered where the emerald had led them.

* * *

"I'm going with you." Eleanor's tone brooked no argument.

"Nora, love—"

"Robin, love." She put her hand over his mouth. "Hush. I'm coming."

"'Twill be dangerous," Robin told her. His arms pulled her onto his chest, his hands sliding down her back to caress her bum. "I don't know for sure if 'tis the green bastard's hideaway or just her own."

"All the more reason for me to come along. Remember what happened the last time we went into his fae world."

"Right." His laugh rumbled through her. His fingers caressed her more.

Eleanor had stowed away on her ex-fiancé's ship, *The Rainbow*, thinking to escape the dreary prospect of becoming no more than an indentured servant in marriage to him. Robin, holding a stolen magic coin, had appropriated the ship with her on it. Desperate to get away from him, Eleanor had nicked the coin and jumped off, swimming to the shore of the nearest island. Robin had followed her, and the coin led them both to an underground fae world, complete with magic and mermaids. It had also been overcast with strong sexual magic that made those who entered it uncontrollably aroused.

"I'm not taking any chances," she told him. "If the emerald takes you to a place like the coin did, I'm not letting you go in there alone."

"Don't tell me you're jealous, love." Robin snuggled her close against his body and nuzzled her neck.

Her nipples tightened against his chest as his teeth grazed her sensitive flesh. "Of that sea-worn hag? Of course not."

He chuckled, sending flames of desire coursing through her. "Are you sure?"

"Under normal circumstances, no." She lifted her head to look at him, then kissed him. She was only partly lying. The pirate queen was sea-worn and though her age was indeterminate, she was far from a hag. "But if the emerald leads you to a place like the one we found before, it won't matter how much I trust you. You wouldn't be able to help yourself."

"And you want to be there to help me instead?" His lips grazed hers. "How considerate of you."

She reached down to pinch his nipple hard enough to make him yelp. "No other wench, pirate captain or no, is going to put her hands on my husband."

"And what of the crew, love? Need I remind you these men are likely to consider rape no more than their just due even without the benefit of fae aphrodisiacs? There will be more of them than of me."

She sighed and tucked her head into the curve of his shoulder. "Don't go without me, Robin. Promise."

He sighed, the deep breath making his chest rise and fall beneath her. "I won't make a promise I don't intend to keep."

She muttered a curse and made to roll off him, but his hands pinned her on top of him. "Don't be angry, love."

She struggled ineffectually in his grip. "I *am* angry! I don't want you going in there alone, and not only because that bloody wee bastard might have put another lust spell on it! I don't want you going in there alone against a whole crew! 'Tis dangerous!"

"Shh, shh, love." His attempts to soothe her made her struggle harder. He pinned her arms at her sides and rolled her beneath him. She couldn't move.

She glared up at him. "Get off me."

He bent to kiss her. She refused to open her mouth. He teased her lips with his. She set hers in a thin, grim line. He moved his mouth along the curve of her jaw to her ear, flicking the sensitive lobe with his tongue before capturing it gently between his teeth. Her nipples tightened again, though she refused to respond. Robin's hand came up to cup one breast, his thumb passing over the taut peak. The sensual caress echoed between her legs, which she kept clamped.

His mouth moved from her ear to her neck and the curve of her shoulder, bared by the scooped neck of her night rail. He nipped her collarbone as he fondled her nipple, rolling it with his fingers.

Heat and hardness pressed on her clit with only the barrier of her cotton gown between them. Robin rocked his pelvis, then nudged one knee between her legs to force them open.

He was too big and too strong…and the things he was doing to her with his mouth and hands almost made her forget she was angry…

She tensed her thighs, but too late. He'd parted her legs and slid between them. When she put her hands against his chest to push at him, he captured both wrists with one large palm and held them above her head.

Now she was well and truly caught. Wiggling only served to rock her body harder against his and cast her night dress into further disarray. Eleanor arched her back, but that only pushed her breasts higher upward—right into Robin's waiting and willing mouth.

Still holding her wrists, he put his mouth to her left nipple. He teased it through the cloth of her gown, wetting the material and blowing his breath across the fabric. Heat, then chill. The delicious and tantalizing combination almost drew a moan from her, but she stifled it by biting her lip.

I'm angry with him!

It was becoming more and more difficult to remember that. He sucked harder on her nipple before moving to the other one to give it the same treatment.

He moved off her slightly, and his free hand caressed her hip. His fingers curled, inching her gown up over her thighs. Baring her to him.

"Don't you dare," Eleanor warned, but got only a chuckle in return. "I'll scream!"

"Go ahead and scream. I'm sure Seamus and Aggie will run to your rescue." He inched her nightgown higher. "'Tis not as though they've never heard me making you scream before."

"Oh!" She gritted her teeth, but couldn't deny the truth of his words.

He kissed lower, down over the curve of her hip. The position made it awkward for him to keep her arms pinned. His grip loosened a bit. "If you really want me to stop, love, I will."

Before she had the chance to reply, he slid his tongue down her belly and straight to her clit. Any protests she'd been meaning to make disappeared under her moan of pleasure.

"Yes?" His tongue stopped its subtle movements. His hot breath caressed her. "You want me to stop?"

"No, Robin!"

She couldn't even find it in herself to be angry at his answering chuckle. He let go of her wrists, and her hands found the top of his head. She wound her fingers in his sun-streaked hair, relishing the texture of it on her palms, belly and thighs.

Robin bent back to tease her clitoris with his tongue, using the tip to make small, precise circles, then the flat of it to lick her more firmly. No matter how many times she'd had his face between her thighs, Eleanor would never tire of this. Robin used his mouth to make love to her more thoroughly and skillfully than many men would have been able to manage with their pricks. Every lick and nibble, every stroke, every carefully directed puff of breath, all had her quivering on the edge of orgasm within moments.

He could have sent her over the edge right away, but Robin preferred to prolong her pleasure. Maddeningly, sometimes. Now, for instance, when he slid a finger inside her to stroke her internally in time to the movements of his tongue.

Eleanor lifted her hips to give him better access, which he took immediate advantage of by adding another finger. He spread them, gently stretching her and rubbing the spot just behind her pubic bone. He fastened his lips on her erect bud, pulling it gently.

Her thighs clenched and relaxed as the first orgasmic contractions began deep in her womb. 'Twas as though she could feel the blood from every part of her body rushing through her veins straight to her center. Her heart pounded and pulse throbbed; light flashed in front of her vision as she let out the breath she'd been holding.

Robin withdrew his fingers and placed one last kiss on her swollen center. He slid his mouth up along her body, capturing her mouth and delving inside.

"Tell me what you want, love."

"You," Eleanor breathed, clutching his rear to pull him closer. "Inside me."

"As you wish."

He filled her with one smooth thrust. They both groaned. He'd propped himself on his hands to enter her, and Eleanor put her hands on his broad, muscled chest. Her fingertips found the pebbled points of his nipples, hard like her own, and she rolled them between her fingers.

"Ah, love—" Robin's words became a moan as she pinched a bit rougher.

He began to move in slow, even strokes and a steady pace she responded to immediately. Her orgasm hovered, the sensation of all her blood flowing to that one point not diminishing. Eleanor matched his thrusts, pressing her clit upward to rub against his belly with every move.

"So slick," Robin murmured. "Neptune's Trident, Nora, 'tis like sinking into butter."

She laughed breathlessly. "How many times have you put your jolly roger into butter, I'd like to know?"

He bent to kiss her. "Never, love. I'm only guessing."

She kissed him, holding onto his back and raking her nails down his skin. "It's all for you, Robin."

His pace quickened. He buried his head in her shoulder. His chest rubbed her breasts, tantalizing the nipples. His pelvis rocked against hers, and her cunny trembled around his length.

"I want to feel your pleasure," Robin said against her neck. "You're so hot, and wet, and tight around my cock. Let go for me, Nora. Let me feel you, love."

With a low cry that soon escalated into a whimper, she gave him what he'd asked for. She let go. Her climax rushed through her, suffusing every digit, every limb, every hair with pure ecstasy. Her entire world became Robin, the hardness of his cock inside her, the tickle of his pubic hair against her throbbing clitoris. The sound of his moan sent waves of pleasure crashing over her.

"Nora!"

She answered with his name, this man she loved. The pure force of her love for him filled her as fully as her orgasm, flooding her entire body with emotion so strong it made tears spring to her eyes. They leaked down her face to puddle near her ears, but she was smiling, not sobbing.

He lifted his head at the touch of wetness. "Nora, love, are you all right?"

"Yes, yes, yes!" She laughed through her tears, her voice shaking as another series of shudders rippled through her.

He thrust harder once, twice, and once more, finally. His heat filled her, and she felt the pounding of his heart against her chest as he sank on top of her.

For a short time, the only sound in the room was their mingled breathing. Eleanor didn't have the strength to speak. Robin rolled off her, but kept her cradled in his arms. She pillowed her head on his chest, feeling his skin cool as the night air dried the sweat. She shivered and pulled up the covers to shield them.

"If we never find the emerald, I wouldn't care," she told him after a while. "Wealth is lovely, Robin, but 'tis not worth so much risk."

"When I made you my wife, I promised to take care of you." Robin's voice was quiet. He stroked her hair. "If I'm to give up pirating, love, we need something to carry us through. I don't mind working, but I don't want my wife to labor. I want to buy you a house overlooking the sea, where you can sit by the window and look pretty."

Eleanor sat up. "Robin Steele! Don't you know anything about me? I've never wanted that! I've never wanted to be only a decoration! 'Tis why I was running away in the first place!"

"Love—"

She cut him off. "Don't you 'love,' me. I want more from life than to be some man's china doll, set up on the mantelpiece and made only to look pretty. I didn't fall in love with you or consent to be your wife for you to risk life and limb going after a treasure you think will take care of us the rest of our lives. Money is nice, Robin, but 'tis nicer when you've earned it."

He sat up, too, his scowl evident even in the dimly lit room. "I'll have earned this treasure, Nora. What's so wrong about me wanting to take care of you? To keep you from trouble?"

"Nothing." She sighed, wanting to reach to touch his face but holding back. "And when we got the emerald, I was as willing as you to seek what it promised. But now Gráinne has it, and getting it back is too much risk. She'll fight you for it, Robin. Is it worth the chance you could be hurt, or even die? She let us off once. She won't be so generous again."

"And 'twas her mistake she let me go," Robin retorted. "She'd have to know I wouldn't let her just take what was mine without seeking retribution. She knows the way of the sea better than that."

"She was merciful," Eleanor spat. "She had you on that plank and gave me your life in exchange for the emerald! There was no question in my mind which I'd choose, and I'd do it again if I had to. Always. Money is nothing to me if I don't have you."

"Nora, love—"

"No, Robin!" She pulled away from his touch. "If you're going to try to convince me of your reasons for finding the emerald, I don't want to hear them. Don't you remember what happened to Winston?"

Even now, the memory made her shudder. Her former fiancé had drowned in quicksand, weighed down by the sack of gold coins he'd found in the leprechaun's lair. His greed had killed him.

"That won't happen to me, love."

"You don't know that," Eleanor cried. "I'm sure Winston didn't think he was going to die when he stepped into that quicksand!"

He tried to soothe her, but she was having none of it. She shrugged off his touch and shrank back against the pillows. He made a disgruntled noise.

"What do you want, Nora? Want me to become a bloody sheep farmer? Do you want me to work in Seamus' stables for the rest of my life, mucking out stalls to keep you fed and clothed?"

"At least 'tis honest work!" The moment the words left her lips she regretted them. "Robin—"

"Belay that. You're right. Pirating is no honest work."

The lilt of his brogue thickened in his anger. He got up from the bed and began to dress, his movements fierce but controlled.

"I didn't mean—"

"You did mean it. And you're right to mean it. I've spent a good portion of my life thieving, Eleanor. I don't regret it, but I do admit it. I'm wanting to make a change. I believe that emerald and what it will lead me to is mine by rights. I intend to get it back. After that, I'll bloody retire to whatever you want me to be, but I'll be damned if I spend the rest of my life slaving in so-called honest work when I know I can provide you with more."

"Don't make this about me. If you want that treasure, want to risk your life for it, don't use me as an excuse! Admit it's for you!"

"There isn't anything I do that isn't for you, Nora." Robin shoved his feet into his boots, then grabbed up his coat and hat. Next he buckled on his pistols. In the light from the fire, he looked imposing and dangerous. He'd let his beard grow again over the past few months, and it framed a mouth gone grim and thin-lipped.

"Gráinne Ni Mhaille stole that emerald from me, and I intend to get it back. 'Tis my hope you'll be here waiting for me when I do."

"Robin—"

"I'm doing this for both of us, and for our wee ones, should the Lord bless us with any. I won't have my wife and children scraping out an existence and living in squalor, never knowing where the next meal will come from, or if the winter'll see them with shoes on their feet. I won't have my wife and children living like my mother did with me."

She wanted to say more, to call him back, but Robin's voice stopped her.

"I know you may not think this is honest work, but 'tis no crime to take back what was yours to begin with. The pirate queen took what was mine. I'm going to get it back."

Before she could say anything else, he'd stormed from the room. The door rocked in its hinges from the force of his slam. Eleanor pulled the covers up around her, chilled from more than just the night air.

"Be safe," she whispered to the empty room. "Damn you, Robin Steele, for your stubbornness!"

* * *

The woman has to be a grandmother already, Robin thought as he watched Gráinne barking orders to her crew. The gray hair and lines on her face attested to that. Yet her back was straight and her voice strong. He'd heard she gave birth to her last son while at sea and under attack and, watching her, Robin didn't find that story difficult to believe. The woman was an Amazon, a warrior, as fierce a pirate captain as any he'd ever known.

But she was also arrogant enough to think him too afraid to come after what she'd stolen from him. Robin had made quite a career of piracy, both along the Irish Coast and in the Caribbean. He'd captained several ships, including the one that had gone down with all his crew aboard. He'd done well, amassing and losing small fortunes, but he'd never gained a reputation for either blood thirstiness or destruction. He'd never earned a nickname like "Black Steele" or "Captain Blood," never had legends told about him. He was a competent pirate—a business man, not a showman. He'd lived the life knowing and not caring that his name was not going to live on in the history books as a scourge of the seas.

That relative anonymity had pleased him. Now it worked for him. Gráinne had let him go, perhaps from mercy as Eleanor had claimed, but more likely because she didn't think she had any reason to fear recrimination. Especially not on her home seas. She was Gráinne Ni Mhaille, after all, Pirate Queen of Connaught, who'd wagered with good Queen Bess herself, and won.

Captain Robin Steele wasn't much compared to that. He counted on that lack of reputation to help him now. She'd never suspect he'd actually come after her, alone against her and a full crew.

Robin took advantage of the night's cover to hide behind one of the large boulders at the cliff base. The tide was low, but the water still swirled and crashed around his legs, trying to pull him into the depths just beyond the rocks. The sea was a harsh mistress, who took what she wanted and raised seven kinds of hell when she didn't get it. Robin wasn't about to taunt the sea tonight. He stayed close to the rock, letting the water tug at him but not moving.

The woman isn't even subtle, he thought as he watched her row toward the shore in a dinghy crewed by five sailors. A lantern at the front of the small boat lit their way, and her ship was as brightly lit as a country squire's gala. She obviously feared no local interference in her plans.

Robin waited until the dinghy pulled up to the narrow, rocky strip of beach at the cliff base. The Cliffs of Moher rose above them hundreds of feet, their craggy vertical surface forbiddingly steep. It had taken him hours to climb down the narrow, crumbling path to get to the bottom. In many places, he'd had to crawl nearly straight down, hands and feet scrabbling for purchase in the cliff face before he could find another spot wide enough to stand on. But he'd made it. Now he watched as the pirate queen, standing, lifted her hands toward the cliffs.

Something glinted, then glowed. Green light seeped through her fingers, and she laughed loud enough for Robin to hear her even over the crashing of the waves. She gestured as one of her crew anchored the dinghy to the rocks. They clambered out, five burly sailors and one surprisingly petite woman.

She shouted something to the crew and lifted the emerald above her head. The green light grew, reflecting off the cliff's barren face. At first, nothing appeared, but as he watched, a thin green line began to glow in the rocks. It made a rectangle. The shape of a door.

Gráinne walked up to the line and passed her hand over it. Her crew backed her up. She held up the emerald, and the doorway's glow responded, but she couldn't seem to be able to figure out how to open it.

"Bloody wee green bastard," Robin muttered with a grin. "You've hexed it shut."

Gráinne waved the emerald again. This time, words appeared in glowing green light above the door's top edge. The Gaelic lettering was difficult for him to see from his vantage point, and Robin took the chance of slipping from behind the rock to get a closer look. The water closed over his head for a few moments as he swam, surfacing near the dinghy and holding onto it to rest himself while he watched the pirate queen and her crew.

"*Is leor nod don eolach.*" Robin read, then chuckled. "A hint is sufficient for the wise. 'Tis a riddle, you wench. Don't tell me you can't figure it out."

This close he could hear her over the sea's complaining.

"A hint," said Grannia as she turned to her men. The emerald's green glow lit her grin. "I think we all know what that means."

Her men winked and nudged each other, guffawing.

"Belay it!" she cried and held up the emerald again. "*Oscail an doras*. Open the door!"

Silently, a space opened in the cliff. Blackness greeted them. Proving her reputation for fearlessness, Gráinne stepped through without hesitation, the emerald hoisted high. Robin saw its green glow light up the passage. Gráinne's curse got the rest of her men moving. Robin swam to the shore, moving as fast as he could without revealing himself.

They weren't even looking. They didn't expect anyone to have followed them. He slipped into the darkness behind them, listening for their footsteps. The glow from the emerald had dimmed; perhaps the passage turned, or they'd gone so far already the light had faded. He put out his hands to the sea-slick walls and felt his way along.

Shouts up ahead made him pause. Silence. He moved forward another few steps. The tunnel did, indeed, curve. He inched his way beyond the turn. From ahead of him another glow reached his eyes, but not green this time.

He grinned. Just like the last place. Robin followed the tunnel walls, each step bringing him closer to the brightness. He listened carefully for any signs Gráinne and her crew were waiting to ambush him.

By the time he got to the end of the tunnel, his clothes were beginning to stiffen against his skin as they dried. The air in the passage was cold and clammy and made him shiver as he peered from the tunnel's edge into the leprechaun's lair.

Unlike the tropical paradise he'd discovered with Nora when they'd followed the pull of the gold coin, this place was as barren and sparse as the cliffs outside. Jutting black rocks covered every inch of the cavern, including the ground. And yet, despite the utter lack of vegetation, the cavern was the loveliest place Robin had ever laid eyes on.

Jewels glittered on every surface. Rubies, emeralds, diamonds, gems of every color and size. Shining sapphires as big as a bird's egg nestled next to chunks of agate and amber.

This place had no fake sky the way the one in the Caribbean had, though, with all the jewels scattered across the ceiling, the effect was nonetheless of a star-strewn night. An unseen light source made all the gems sparkle and reflected off them to make the entire space glow with a brilliance that could blind a man who wasn't careful to shield his eyes.

Robin squinted, hand up to do just that. *The first of the wee bastard's tricks,* he thought. Blind any trespassers with promised glory, so they don't bother to move forward. In the next moment, his thought was proven correct. One of Gráinne's crew stood, frozen, his hand on one immense ruby sticking out from the wall. Blood poured from his eyes, nose and ears. His mouth gaped in silent agony.

Robin gave him wide berth. This was not the treasure, only a glamor to keep the greedy from venturing further. He kept moving.

The cavern widened as he moved cautiously, listening for those who'd gone ahead. Every once in a while he heard an echoed shout that told him he was going in the right direction. By now the place had grown so much he could no longer see the sides of it, or the ceiling. The glow still suffused the space, giving him light enough to see, and the floor still glittered with broken gemstones. He ignored them and kept walking.

The floor became black sand that sucked at and clung to his still-damp boots. Footprints dented it, and he followed them. The cavern narrowed again, and the gems became scarcer. Another trick, he saw when he came upon another of Gráinne's crew in the same condition as his mate.

"Brilliant wee bugger," Robin said aloud, looking around. "Make us think 'tis our last chance to get the treasure."

He knew better, and apparently so did Gráinne, for she'd continued to lead the way through one more tunnel. This one ended in a large cavern lit with more of the same diffuse light.

How much time had passed since he'd entered the tunnel? It didn't feel like hours, but Robin knew well how time passed in the fae realm. Not like it did in the mortal world. Had he been here days? Would Nora be worried?

The screams distracted him, and he jumped, looking around for the source. A woman's voice—but furious, not scared. Gráinne?

Just ahead of him was a small pool of black water, fed by a trickle from a cluster of large boulders. The scream had come from behind it. He made his hasty way there. What he saw made him stop dead in his tracks.

Gráinne stood on top of a big, flat rock, her sword in one hand and a knife in the other. Her shirt and vest had been torn in the back, exposing a good part of her skin. Her eyes blazed with fury, her grayed hair had come undone from its braid. Her crew members were leaping at her, their gibbering and lewd grins making their intentions clear.

The moment Robin stepped beyond the boulder barrier, he understood why. His cock rose into a sudden, painful erection, so fierce he had to stop and put his hand on the rocks to keep from falling. All at once, he could smell her: woman. Female. Goddess. His nostrils flared and all he could think of was plunging his aching flesh into slick heat, sating his lust, spewing his seed…

"Bloody bollocks," he cursed, wrenching upright and shaking himself. "Magic, Robin, 'tis what's got your prick at full mast. Naught more."

"Away with ye, ye bloody great bastards!" Gráinne hollered, swiping at the three sailors with her sword. "To hell I'll send you if you touch me again!"

"Ah, shut your gob," cried one. "Open your legs instead!"

His comrades laughed.

"Aye," cried another. "Spread for us, Gráinne! Show us you're not the dried up, old twat you pretend to be!"

Gráinne spat down into his face. "As if I'd care to lie beneath the likes of you, Finley! I've seen what you piss with, remember?"

Finley growled and danced forward, but Gráinne slapped him back with the flat of her sword. "Bugger off!"

She didn't seem particularly afraid. Furious and perhaps a bit amused. Robin had to admire the woman's courage, but then he supposed a woman used to captaining an entire crew of men had to be able to defend herself.

The third man hadn't said anything, concentrating his efforts on sneaking around behind her. He leaped up on the rock with a yell. Gráinne turned, knife flashing, but 'twas too late. He'd grabbed her about the waist, pinning her sword arm. The knife flashed again, slicing his arm, but the pirate grabbed her by the back of her hair while the other two men jumped up on the rock.

"Feargal, you great bloody git! Let me go!"

"Grab her, Francis," cried Feargal, struggling to hold her.

The woman might be a thief and a rival, but there was no way Robin was going to stand by and watch her be raped by members of her own crew. With an echoing shout, he sprang out of hiding, wishing he'd been able to bring his pistols. He'd left them tucked into a crevice, wrapped in oilcloth to protect them from the spray and rising tide. He did have two blades, however, which he whirled with both hands over and over in a figure eight pattern designed to intimidate as well as defend.

"Where the bloody hell did he come from?" cried Finley.

Feargal grunted. "Who cares? Finish him!"

Francis ran at Robin with a grin so wide and eyes glinting so gleefully Robin didn't doubt the pirate intended to fuck him and then kill him, if not the other way 'round. He stood his ground, knives stilled for the moment.

With a roar, the man launched himself at Robin, who side-stepped the attack. "Hard to run with your cock like a shaft of iron, eh, mate?"

Francis had slammed into the boulders and fallen. He got up, shaking his head, fury like a dark cloud on his face. "You'll pay for that, bucko."

"I think not," was Robin's mild reply, as he neatly side-stepped the man again.

Neptune's balls, his own prick was chafing fiercely inside his pants, but at least he knew this sudden arousal for what it was—magic.

"Listen, mate," Robin said. "You don't need to do this. It's the bloody leprechaun who's done it. You don't need—"

With another roar, the man had launched himself again. This time, his flailing fists caught Robin on the shoulder. But Robin's left-hand knife tore through the pirate's sleeve and nicked the skin. Blood spurted. The pirate cursed, holding his arm.

"Difficult to think about fucking when you're leaking that way," said Robin. "Best patch that up, boyo."

He looked over to where the other two men had pinned Gráinne down. Finley watched as Feargal shoved his trousers down to his ankles and poised himself between the pirate queen's legs.

"Ah, now, mate, you don't want to be doing that," Robin cried, running toward them.

He didn't need to bother. Gráinne proved, once again, she could take care of herself. Though her arms had been pinned at her sides, she bucked upward with her hips, throwing off her attacker. With a triumphant scream, she rolled over and stabbed Feargal in the chest. He gave a burbling cry and began to twitch. She got to her feet and shoved the stunned-looking Finley off the rock. He struck his head on the ground and lay still.

"You next?" Her bared teeth were more feral than female. She held up the bloodstained blade. "Come on then."

"No, madame. I'm interested in the treasure to be found in this cavern, not the one betwixt your thighs." Robin kept his eye on the still-bleeding pirate, who'd bound his arm with strips of his shirt, but had sunk, ashen-faced to the ground.

"The mast in your pants tells me otherwise," said Gráinne. "And 'tis just as unlikely for me to give up the fae man's treasure as it is for me to give you my own. So bugger off."

"I can't do that," Robin answered, moving closer, his own knives ready. "That emerald belongs to me, and I'll have it, if you please."

"It does not please me, laddie," said Gráinne with a smirk. She brushed her hair back from her face.

"Mayhap 'twould please you better should I let them have another go at you?"

Gránnie laughed. "You act as though I needed your help."

"Mayhap not, but I gave it," Robin pointed out.

She came closer and put her hand to his cheek. "I know you."

"Get your hands off him!"

Robin was pleased to see the woman, could indeed, be startled, but he was just as stunned. They both turned.

"Nora!"

"You keep your hands off him, you strumpet!" Nora brandished a pistol Robin didn't recognize. "And you, you scurvy seadog! What do you think you're doing?"

"This is your woman?" Gráinne asked mildly. "She's a real fireball."

"Shut your gob," said Nora smartly. "And give me the emerald, else I'll blow your brains to bits."

"She won't," said Gráinne.

"She might," said Robin conversationally. He shrugged. "She looks well and sorely furious to me."

"I am!" Nora waved the gun again. "You bloody bastard."

"Ah, *leannán*. Don't take on so. 'Tis no way to treat your man." Gráinne grinned.

Nora didn't return the smile. "Give me the emerald."

"I don't think so, *leannán*."

"I'm not your sweetheart." Nora carefully cocked the gun. The sound seemed very loud in the cavern. Even Robin's heart beat a bit faster in anticipation.

"You'd best do as she says," Robin advised. "She's not a pirate."

"And what does that mean?" Nora demanded, her eyes wavering from her target for a moment.

"It means you don't live by the code, and therefore can't be trusted," said Gráinne.

Nora's face grew stony, but while she was not a pirate, Gráinne definitely was. The older woman took immediate advantage of Nora's slip of attention. She leaped off her rock, hollering, knife flying.

Nora ducked. Robin was quicker. He bent his shoulder and rammed into Gráinne as hard as he could. Her breath whooshed out of her and she began to topple. At the same time, though, she brought the hilt of her weapon up under his chin.

"Look at the stars," Robin managed to say through the taste of blood in his mouth, and then darkness overtook him.

* * *

Robin groaned and wriggled beside her. Eleanor shifted her weight to release some of the tension in her arms. He'd been asleep for so long, dead weight against her, that her limbs had gone numb.

Finding the entrance to the cavern would have seemed like blind luck had she not been searching so hard. The grass on top of the cliff was wild, thick and green, luxurious. The perfect place to hide an entrance to a fae realm.

Seamus from the inn had told her what to look for. "Ye seeking Ricky of the Tuft, lass? Ye might find him on top of the cliffs. Find the fae circle." He'd laughed. "If ye dare."

She'd dared, and hadn't bothered to tell the innkeeper she wasn't interested in Ricky of the Tuft, but instead some wee green man and a pirate queen, a stolen emerald and her husband.

The mound had looked innocent enough, and hidden so well in the verdant growth she'd nearly tumbled headfirst into it. The tunnel inside was narrow, steep and treacherous, but the thought of Robin kept her going until at last she'd ended up coming out into the cavern, where she saw Gráinne and Robin fighting.

She didn't know how they'd managed to find their way inside, but judging by their clothes it had been a much more arduous journey than her own.

"Nora?"

"I'm here."

"Neptune's balls," Robin said. "I think the sea bitch broke my bloody jaw."

"Be glad I didn't do worse." Eleanor tried to make her voice harsh, but failed.

"Where are we?"

"Tied up in the cavern while that hoyden and her minions gather the treasure."

Robin made a disgusted noise. "They found it then."

"Oh, aye. They found it." Eleanor grumbled. "Vast hordes of it, if you can tell anything by their cries. This after she threatened to castrate any of them who touched her again."

She shifted. The sand under her bottom was soft but cold. The pirate queen had tied them up, back to back, wrists bound between them. The ropes had loosened over the hours she'd been tugging at them, but Robin being unconscious had meant she could do little more.

"Did they hurt you?" he whispered fiercely into the darkness.

"No. She kept them from that." Eleanor shivered at the thought of what those rough men were capable of even when not crazed by the fae lust spell.

"Because he's put it here, too. Just like in the Caribbean." Robin took a deep breath that lifted his shoulders. "My cock is like rock."

She laughed at the play on words. "Indeed."

Robin wiggled more. "But even despite that, love, I'd not have touched her."

"I know that."

She did, too. Eleanor moved against him. Her nipples had peaked against the linen of the shirt she'd borrowed from him. She'd also nicked a pair of his trousers, and the seam at the crotch rubbed against her with every wiggle.

"I've been sitting here in the dark for hours listening to you breathe," she murmured. "And smelling you. Even if not for the leprechaun's magic I'd be in a frenzy of wanting."

He groaned and tilted his head back to touch hers. His long hair drifted over her shoulders, tickling her cheek. She turned her face to let it caress her lips.

"I've oft dreamed about having you bound." Robin chuckled wryly. "But not quite like this."

"You haven't," she breathed, the thought suddenly exciting her beyond imagination.

A few muffled shouts from Gráinne's crew made Robin mutter a curse. Eleanor grinned into the darkness.

"Who? Them or me?" she replied to his choice of words.

"You," Robin said. "And then I'll take care of them."

She laughed. "You'll have to get free of these ropes first."

"I can't think of any better reason to do it." He moved against her again. "But the question is, love, how?"

She moved her wrists, where the ropes were still tight, then wiggled her back. The ropes around their bodies had loosened, as had the ropes around her ankles.

"Press hard against me and we can rise up."

Robin laughed. "I always rise up when I press hard against you, love."

Another round of shouts and clangs, closer this time, made her shake her head. "Don't you think we should concentrate on getting free before they finish with the treasure and come back for us?"

"Right, love. Here we go."

The pressure grew against her back, and Eleanor pushed her feet against the ground, forcing herself against his back and using the leverage to slowly stand.

"Brilliant," Robin told her. "I knew you'd come up with something."

Now they stood, back to back.

"We should be able to turn and face each other now."

They did, hopping inelegantly in a circle until they were chest to chest.

"What now?"

Eleanor cocked her head to listen for more sounds from Gráinne's crew. "Let me try to pull free."

She bent her knees, trying to duck down through the ropes tying them together. She got as far as his waist before the rope no longer stretched enough. It had caught on her shoulders and at her head.

"Won't work," she said.

Robin's voice was rough. "That works for me."

She rubbed her face against his hardness, desire coursing through her veins. The leprechaun's magic was part of it, but most of it was him. Her Robin. Her husband. Her love.

It wasn't the most appropriate time for lovemaking. Her body didn't care. She moved up along his body again, the ropes making her keep close. His erection nudged her stomach.

"This isn't the time," she said.

"I know." Robin's voice sounded like a smile. "Blame it on the wee green bugger."

"What now?"

"If you move around a bit, maybe I can reach your wrists."

She tried. He helped. But the uneven ground and their bound feet made for imbalance. "Robin!"

He managed to break their fall by twisting to the side, but her wind still got knocked out of her. She ended up on top of him.

"I think the ropes are loose enough now." His voice was strained, whether from the fall or arousal, she couldn't tell.

She inched her body up along his until she could reach his face. She brushed her lips along his. He responded by capturing her mouth with his. His tongue delved inside, stroking.

"We don't have time for this, Robin."

"You're right, love."

He kissed her again and suddenly she felt his arms around her. "You're free!"

He chuckled, his hands roaming. "How much time do you think we have?"

"Long enough, I think, if you can be quick."

"The way I'm feeling, I'll have to be quick."

He untied her swiftly, his mouth devouring as much of her as he could reach. Cheeks, forehead, chin, neck, jaw, lips, down to the curve to her collarbone, nibbling. Down lower, to the first swell of her breasts as he flipped her onto her back and dove between her legs.

Thank Neptune the sand's soft, she thought as her shirt rucked up and her trousers came down. In the next second, he entered her. She bit back a scream.

Yes, it was the magic that made them so mad for one another, but not solely that. She was always ready for him, always eager. Always wanted him.

Even now, knowing that at any moment Gráinne and her crew could come back for them only made the heat between them hotter. He thrust in smooth, even strokes, filling her, holding her against him. His kisses burned along her skin. His tongue left wet paths on her skin. She bit at him and dug her nails into his back, urging him harder. Faster.

"Nora!" Robin's cry echoed around her, plunging her into ecstasy.

Her orgasm crashed over her, fierce as an ocean storm. She surged and crested with it. She shattered beneath it, then merged again in the aftermath.

Breathing hard, Robin shuddered his own release. He gathered her into his arms, holding her tightly and kissing her breathless.

"Neptune's balls," he whispered. "I could take you again right now."

"Magic," Eleanor whispered back.

"I know it," Robin replied, moving inside her again. "But it's also you, love."

"Isn't this a pretty sight?" Gráinne's voice and the light from her lantern made Eleanor turn. "I've half a mind take a turn at him meself, lass. I'm as on edge as a virgin on her wedding night, only not as scared. Something about this place."

Robin covered Eleanor with his body until she could pull her clothes around her. The two of them got up. He put his arm around her.

"We've done naught to you," Robin said. "Just take the treasure and leave us alone."

Gráinne shook her head. "Sure, and I could do that, could I not? Let you go to haunt my footsteps again? I don't think so, laddie. I might not have much time left in this world, but what I do have, I intend not to spend looking over my shoulder for the likes of you."

"You'll spend the rest of your life looking over your shoulder because of what you do," Eleanor said.

Gráinne opened her palm and held out a handful of jewels. "Not with these, I won't. I'm going to take this treasure and retire from the sea. 'Tis time I dandled grandbabies on my knees instead of swashbuckling."

"So you'll kill us?" Eleanor cried, astounded. "In one breath you speak of children, while in the next you condemn us to die?"

Gráinne shrugged. "Yon lad is a pirate, same as me. He won't rest until he's taken what I took from him."

"Not true," Eleanor argued, but a look from Robin stopped her. She frowned. "Robin?"

"She's right, Nora." Robin straightened his back. "But I ask you give us the choice."

The pirate queen gave him a shrewd look. "Become food for the fish or hang from the mast?"

"I was hoping for abandonment," Robin told her.

Eleanor's looked at the other woman. "What?"

Gráinne looked her over. "Laddie wants me to leave the pair of you here to starve to death. We'll block the entrance up after we go. Leave you a pistol with two shots for when the pains get too fierce. Ahh, a true lover's death." She peered more closely at Robin. "You really want to see your lady fair suffer so? Does she get cranky when her belly's empty? Seek ye to fill her womb with your seed a few more times before you leave this earth?"

Eleanor looked at Robin for an explanation, but his eyes had locked on Gráinne. "Aye, lady captain. I do. I love this woman more than my own life, and would be glad of whatever time with her I'm granted, no matter how short."

Gráinne's face softened for a moment. "Ah, lad, you remind me of me of someone I once knew." For an instant 'twas as though tears glinted in her eyes, but the light was so dim and shifting Eleanor couldn't be sure. "I'll give you your abandonment."

"Neptune's blessings on you, lady captain." Robin inclined his head, his arm tight around Eleanor's shoulder.

"Ahoy!" shouted Gráinne toward the rest of her crew. "Avast and away, you scurvy swabbies! Carry what you can and let's be gone. I want the stink of this place out of my nostrils."

She turned back to Robin and Eleanor. "I'll be sealing up the doorway on the way out, not to mention 'tis likely you won't be able to open it without the emerald anyway. I know how the fae work. But just in case, I'll be filling it with rubble. At any rate, you've got water. Plenty of air. 'Tis not too cold. You could live a good fortnight before madness drives you to take the bullet."

"You're too kind." Eleanor glared.

Gráinne only smiled. "Ah, me lovely, kind is one thing I've never claimed to be. Foolhardy and sentimental on occasion, and merciful when it suits me. But never kind."

"Ready to go, cap'n," said Francis. He'd bound his arm with strips of cloth. His pockets bulged, as did the sack made from the remnants of his shirt.

Gráinne nodded. "Funny how the promise of castration can even overpower a fae fuck glamor."

The crewman looked chastened, his sheepish grin revealing missing teeth. "Begging your pardon, cap'n. We couldn't help ourselves."

"God's teeth," Gráinne replied. "As if I don't know it meself. If the thought of taking all of you didn't make my stomach sick, I'd have gladly done it. You, on the other hand," she said to Robin, "would've been a delicious treat. Or even you, lass, should I have fancied tasting Sappho's nectar."

Eleanor frowned and started to retort, but Robin's hand on her arm stopped her.

"And under other circumstance, the pleasure would have been mine," said Robin gallantly. "But my heart belongs to this lady."

Gráinne threw back her head, her laughter echoing around the cavern. "I didn't want your heart, laddie, only your prick. Never mind. 'Tis well. Passions of the flesh are well and good, but they can't keep you fed or clothed. What I'll take away with me today will do that, and tenfold."

"Indeed."

Robin's smug smile infuriated Eleanor, for though she'd argued he didn't need to chase after the pirate queen to get back the emerald, he had. And now, for what? Nothing, in the end. And he was courting her like a young swain to an elderly but generous dowager patroness.

Gráinne flashed Nora a smile. "Anon, gentle lady. You should've stayed in your place."

"My place is at Robin's side."

Gráinne shrugged. "And there you'll be when you're both dead as well. Good luck with that."

Eleanor almost launched herself at the older woman, but Robin's gentle touch held her back. She watched in fury as Gráinne slung several bulging sacks over her shoulders and hefted a small cask brimming with jewels.

"Anon, my lovely lad and lassie," she said with a jerk of her chin toward the crewmen. "You'll find the pistol high up on that crag. Two shots. Finley, tie them hard enough to keep them occupied for a bit, but no so hard they'll not get free."

Finley did so quickly, then gathered his own booty. Grannia smiled and shouted orders to her crew, then led them away through the standing rocks.

"I hope you have a plan," Eleanor said when the pirates had disappeared.

Robin's deep chuckle made the fine hairs on the back of her neck rise. "Always, love. Always."

* * *

Finley had been a bit too generous with his rope tying, but nevertheless they'd freed themselves. By that time, Robin's stomach had started growling. His wrists were chafed. And yet the first thing he did when they wiggled free of their bonds was to take Nora in his arms and kiss her thoroughly.

She responded, her tongue dipping into his mouth where he stroked it with his. "What's your brilliant plan?"

He pulled away, arms still around her. "You trust I have one?"

"Of course I do." She smiled, far less angry than he was expecting.

He grinned and kissed her again. "You don't believe we'll be trapped inside here to starve to death?"

"No." She stood on her toes to kiss him again, softer this time. "Though I'm sorry we've lost the treasure again."

"But we haven't, love." Robin grinned at her, running his hands over her tangled hair. "Do you not remember what happened to us the first time?"

She tilted her head to look at him, an eyebrow raised. "Winston took the coins with him into the quicksand."

"But what else, love?" He took her hand and led her toward the place Gráinne and the sailors had been plundering. "What was she carrying when she left?"

"Sacks filled with jewels." Nora thought for a moment. "A cask, also filled."

"And look where they got it from." Robin pointed to the overlarge trunk, its lid gaping, but the interior empty. "Does it look familiar?"

Nora began to laugh, stepping closer to run her hands along the lid. "The trunk. Just like the one in the other place." She laughed louder, closed the lid and said, "Shepherd's pie with a side of steamed greens."

The smell of the food made his stomach grumble even louder when she pulled out the tray. "The magic trunk that gives you whatever you want. Gráinne wanted the treasure, and that's what she got."

Nora held the food to her nose and sniffed, her expression ecstatic. "And anything that come from the magic trunk—"

"Can't be taken out of the realm." Robin laughed. "Methinks the lady captain will be quite disappointed when she gets back on board and finds her bags empty and the entrance permanently closed off."

Nora joined his laughter. "You're bloody brilliant, Robin. But how did you know?"

"Because there is no way the wee green bastard would've made it that easy." He grinned, reaching into the trunk and pulling out two mugs of ale. "And because I knew there was no way you'd climbed down those cliffs to get in, so there had to be another door we could use to escape. And because I know Gráinne Ni Mhaille has had so many triumphs 'twould not occur to her that she might possibly fail."

Nora knelt next to the steaming meat pastry and pulled it apart, exposing the succulent chunks of meat inside the crust. She waved to disperse the steam, then scooped a bit of gravy onto a hunk of brown bread. She gave a low moan of appreciation when she popped it into her mouth.

"Delicious," she murmured. "This, at least, is real enough."

"In here, yes." Robin sat next to her and helped himself. "And when we've sated this hunger, we'll look for the real treasure."

"And what of the other hunger?" she asked him archly. "The magic's as strong in here as it was before. Or mayhap I simply want you for my own reasons."

He leaned over to kiss her. "Insatiable wench."

She put her arms on his shoulders and wound her fingers through his hair, tugging it. "Insatiable means unable to be sated. I think you should at least attempt to sate me, Robin, before you make such a judgment."

The food was forgotten as he pulled her onto his lap, pressing her down on the erection that had never really gone away since he'd entered the cavern.

"If we could put this air into a tincture, we'd need no treasure. We'd only have to sell it to young women with old husbands, and old men wed to young wives." He rocked her gently against his cock, loving the way her breath caught in her throat. "A potion to provide ever-present tumescence."

She laughed low in her throat and brushed her lips along his jaw. "I think 'tis better we don't. Nobody would ever get any work done."

"But imagine how merry everyone would be." He slid his hands to the curve of her buttocks, cupping the firm globes.

His mouth sought hers, and he teased her lips with feather-light flicks of his tongue before plunging inside to taste her. The rich taste of lamb and spices mingled with her own fresh flavor, sending his cock surging even harder against her. His trousers chafed uncomfortably, the pressure making him shift. Nora pressed her center to him as her breathing got faster.

"I can't get enough of you, Nora."

"Nor I, you." She sighed, letting her head tilt back to thrust her breasts upward toward his waiting mouth. "I want you inside me, Robin."

He groaned at the thought and captured one erect nipple through the cloth of her shirt. He moved her hips, rubbing her against him, before pulling the shirt up and over her head. She wore only a sheer binding cloth beneath, and that was quickly unwound. Again he dipped his head to take one nipple and then the other between his lips, suckling.

She moaned. Quickly he shifted her, laying her down on the soft sand floor and covering her breasts with kisses while he loosened his trousers. His erection sprang free as he kicked off the garment and tugged off his shirt. His tongue lingered in the shallow cup of her naval while he nudged her trousers down past her hips and found her clitoris with his tongue.

"Robin!"

He knelt between her legs, mindful of the sand beneath them and not wanting to scrape against it. He sampled her, the sweet warmth of her juices an aphrodisiac that made his already straining cock throb.

When the first flutter of her climax tickled his lips, he paused his stroking tongue to press it flat against her. She arched upward, crying out, convulsing under his mouth.

When she relaxed, he moved up along her body and slid the tip of his prick along her slick folds, seeking entrance into her moist tunnel. Nora opened her eyes, her cheeks flushed and her mouth smiling. She reached for him, pulled him closer. He slid inside her.

They both moaned. He propped himself on his arms so as not to crush her, then began to move. Slow, steady thrusts he knew would please her, adding a small twist of his hips each time to stimulate her center. Her cunny enfolded him, enclosed and engulfed him. He'd never been with a woman who could take all of him the way his Nora could. She hooked her ankles around the back of his legs and dug her nails into his back, urging him on with wordless cries.

His pace quickened as his balls tightened, filling with his seed. Nora quivered around him, her soft cry letting him know she'd reached another climax. Robin's cock felt huge, like it had taken over his entire body. In a way, it had. There was no other sensation than the slick inferno of Nora's cunt gripping him, or the weight of his testicles moving as he thrust.

She scored his back once more with her fingernails, her cry echoing all around him and sending him hurtling past his last resistance and into orgasm.

He thrust inside her once more, to the hilt, hard enough to move them both along the sand. "Nora!"

After a moment she began to laugh, and he lifted his head. "What's so merry?"

"I'll carry the evidence of this for some days," she said. "In the brush burns on my back."

Quickly he gathered her up, cradling her and brushing the sand from her skin. "I'm sorry, love."

She shook her head, snuggling close to him for a moment. "'Tis no worry. I'll survive. And any time they twinge, I'll remember this and want you all over again."

"By Neptune, I love you." He kissed her.

"And I love you." She kissed him, then looked around. "But I think I shall go and avail myself of that water now. Then we'll finish our food, for I'm fair starving. And after that, I propose we find the real treasure and get ourselves out of this place."

"Agreed." He kissed the tip of her nose and brushed her hair off her face. "To all of what you just said."

"You are not the only one who can make plans," Nora replied and chucked his chin before getting off his lap.

"But that's what I love about you," he called after her as she walked toward the pool of black water. "You're so bloody brilliant!"

* * *

Bodies clean and bellies filled, Eleanor and Robin set to work looking for the real treasure.

"It won't be as obvious as that trunk," Robin said.

Eleanor looked around. "I must say, I enjoyed his other paradise more. This place is neither inviting nor pleasant."

She looked upward. "In fact, the only nice aspect of this place is the light. Imagine if it were as dark as a real cavern would be."

"Fae light," Robin scoffed. "Bad for the eyes."

She slipped her arm around his waist. "Oh, I don't know. 'Tis extremely flattering."

He kissed her. "Are you telling me you only find me handsome in dim light?"

She laughed and shook her head at his obvious fishing for a compliment. "Of course. In the light of day, 'tis too easy to see all your faults."

He growled, but then laughed. "Fair enough."

"Where should we look first?" Eleanor scanned the cavern walls. In this part, they were closer together, the ceiling lower. "It could be anywhere. If 'tis even in this part. And without the emerald to guide us—"

"We don't need the emerald. And 'tis here. The other parts of the cavern were rigged to trap the greedy or impatient. Any who make it this far are worthy of finding the treasure, should they not be fooled by the magic trunk and seek the true bounty."

"And we weren't fooled." She grinned at the thought of Gráinne's screams of fury. "She must've discovered the truth by now."

"Aye." Robin laughed and hugged her. "And she'll have no one to blame but herself."

"That doesn't solve the problem of finding it now."

Robin nodded, and she took in the sight of him. He'd rebraided his long hair and tied it with a hank of leather string. His short beard framed the mouth she so loved to kiss. He'd pulled on his trousers and shirt, but left the collar unlaced to reveal tantalizing glimpses of bare, muscled chest...

"If you keep looking at me that way, I'll be forced to make love to you again."

She smiled. "I'll hold you to it."

He moved to pull her into his arms, but she found the strength to resist him. "Powerful magic, Robin. I'm sure he puts it here to keep us so distracted we forget to look for the treasure."

"You're right." Robin grinned unabashedly. "Bloody green bugger."

"Look for the treasure," she said sternly. "I'd like to see the sun again."

"Aye, aye, cap'n." Robin grinned and sauntered away.

She watched him go, admiring the way the muscles of his rear bunched and rolled in his tight trousers...she shook herself. Powerful magic, indeed! With a chuckle, Eleanor began looking around.

In the end, 'twas deceptively simple. Robin had described the glittering gems lodged into the stone walls on his way into this cavern, but Eleanor knew enough about gemstones to remember an important fact. Jewels did not shine or glitter until they'd been cut and polished. Diamonds and rubies, emeralds, sapphires, all looked much the same before the hand of the jeweler revealed their glory.

"Those jewels are only more fae glamor," she said aloud. "Real jewels aren't so pretty. 'Tis the rocks," she said aloud, looking around. They were everywhere, scattered on the floor, overflowing crevices, jumbled in piles. "Robin, the rocks!"

He stopped where he stood, bent to pick up a dull gray stone. He rubbed it with the hem of his shirt until it gleamed faintly red "'Twas all around us the entire time."

"Gráinne was so focused on seeing what she thought was treasure, she failed to see the truth." Eleanor laughed aloud and ran to hug him, dancing.

"Bloody brilliant woman," Robin murmured, kissing her. "Let's get back into the sunshine, love."

Together, they gathered as many stones as they could fit in their pockets and in the sack made from Robin's shirt. They left many lay were there, mindful of how greed had ended Winston Dandrew's life. Even so, the number they took would ensure their comfort for the rest of their lives, as well as their children's.

Children, Eleanor thought suddenly with a secret smile. *Yes. Someday.* She slanted a glance at Robin, imagining a lad with her dark hair and Robin's easy smile. A lass with curls the color of Robin's wheat hair and her green eyes.

"What are you smiling about, love?"

She patted her bulging pockets. "The future."

She led him to the opening that led to the surface. "'Twill be quite a climb."

"Are you up for it?" he asked.

"I made it down. I'll make it back up."

He grinned and kissed her. "I'm going to buy you the most comfortable house you've ever seen, with servants to cater to your every whim."

"I don't need servants. Not so long as I have you."

He kissed her again, so fiercely it took away her breath. "I'll climb up first and reach down for you."

He did, clambering up the rocks as nimbly as a monkey. As Eleanor waited for him to wedge himself into the opening and reach a hand for her to grab, something caught the corner of her eye. A wide band of gold glittered in the dark sand. She picked it up. A ring, just the size to fit loosely on her middle finger, and carved with symbols she didn't recognize. Perhaps Gráinne had dropped it. It looked like the sort of primitive ornament the pirate queen would favor.

"Ready, love?"

"Ready!"

She reached for his hand. His fingers clasped her wrist and hauled her upward into the tunnel. There were few hand or foot holds, but the space was narrow enough they could lever themselves upward by pressing their backs against one side and their feet against the other.

At least, they could at first. As long as the tunnel sloped gently, and they could take breaks. At last they reached a point where the passage took a sharp turn almost directly up. Brush and grasses grew along the sides, proving the sun reached it. They were very close to the top. And yet...

"I'm not sure I can manage," she panted, ashamed of her weakness, but unable to help it.

Her legs quivered with exhaustion from hours of hard use, and every muscle ached. Her back, already scraped by the sand during their lovemaking, now felt rubbed to rawness. Every inch she moved upward took more effort than she was sure she had...and at any moment she feared she'd begin sliding backward. At this point, that fall would mean injury, if not death.

"Empty your pockets," Robin said. "You're carrying too much weight."

"But—"

"Empty them, Nora!" His voice was firm. "I'll not have my wife tumble down to her death for the sake of a pocket of rocks."

She nodded, grateful and disappointed at the same time. With weary, trembling fingers she dumped her pockets. Together they listened to the clatter and thud as the gems tumbled down the shaft into the darkness below.

"Can you make it just a bit further, love?"

She nodded, tears of weariness threatening to blur her vision. With the gems gone, her legs still ached, but her body felt so much lighter. "Yes."

"Good. Because we're almost there."

They inched their way upward a bit more, wedging themselves tightly against the passage.

"I can smell the sea," Robin said. "And it must be night, for I believe I can see the winking of the stars."

She'd grown so accustomed to crawling through pitch blackness that, even when she strained her eyes, she couldn't see anything but black. "I'm so tired, Robin."

"I know, love. Just a bit more."

Eleanor forced herself to gather strength. She heard him exclaim, but the sound of her breath had grown so loud in her ears she wasn't sure what he said. She pushed upward with her legs, and the pain in her back became agony as the raw skin tore against the rocks.

"Robin!" she screamed as she felt herself giving way. Falling. Her body tensed in preparation, trying to grab onto any outcropping, any hold—

And he caught her. Together they slid a few feet before his legs slammed tight against the tunnel wall and stopped their fall. His hands gripped the shoulder of her shirt. The soft purr of ripping cloth caught her attention.

"I've got you!" he cried, his grip tightening on her body, fingers digging into her.

She slipped another inch then stopped. Sobs of terror burst out of her, but she stifled them quickly. She couldn't afford to be shaking now. She reached upward, clutching at his wrists.

"Shake out my pockets, love."

She didn't argue, though the thought of losing the rest of the gems made her sick. The stones scattered over her, catching in her hair and on her clothes before most of them fell down the shaft.

"I'm going to pull you up with me, love. One step at a time."

They moved together, pushing and pulling. Now Eleanor could smell the sea and realized she could see the Robin silhouetted above her in starlight. She gasped the fresh air gratefully.

"I'm at the top, love. I'm going to climb out, then reach for you. Can you hold on until then?"

Smelling the air and knowing they were so close gave her strength. "Yes."

"Good."

She heard him scramble out of the hole. Then she saw the dark shape of his head looking down at her. "Reach up and grab my hand, love."

She did, her shoulders screaming as she stretched the abused muscles. Robin grabbed her wrist. She moved her feet, pushing upward. She was almost out.

At the last moment, the edge of the hole began to give way. She slid down, Robin following. Dirt and rock cascaded over her, gritting in her eyes, clogging her nose, choking her throat. The bag of gems they'd made from Robin's shirt fell forward, striking the side of her face and making her cry out. She reached up, blindly, trying to grab hold of anything that would save her. She found his braid.

"Hold on!" Robin's voice gave her strength. He stopped her fall, and then he was pulling her up and out, her body scraping agonizingly against the sides of the tunnel, but Eleanor didn't care.

The bag fell past her and disappeared, but in the next moment she was safe in his arms, with grass all around them and the sea breeze washing over them. She sobbed in relief, never so glad to feel solid, unyielding ground in her life.

"I've got you, love," Robin soothed her, stroking her hair. "I've got you."

They lay like that for some long moments while the moon rose in the sky. At last she sat up, every movement stiff…but at least she was capable of moving at all.

"We lost it all," she said.

"No, love." Robin sat up and curled her to him. "We still have each other, and 'tis all that matters."

He reached into his pocket. "And I've got a few stones left. Surely they'll provide us with a few weeks' bread and ale."

She managed a laugh, reaching up to touch his face. As she did, the ring she'd found glinted in the moonlight. She looked at it, turning it one way and the other.

"Robin?" She got to her feet, holding out her hand first toward the land, then toward the sea.

"Yes, love?"

As she turned, her hand like the needle of a compass, the tingle on her finger made her laugh out loud and shake her head. "I don't think we're done just yet."

He stood and took her hand, peering down at the ring. "Where'd you find this?"

"Down there." She laughed again, giddy from the combined effects of fear and overwhelming weariness.

"'Tis covered with Egyptian hieroglyphics." Robin stroked the metal with his thumb. "'Tis burning you, is it not?"

She nodded, a giddy grin on her face. "What do you say, Captain Steele?"

"I say, Mrs. Steele," said Robin, pulling her into his arms for a kiss, "we find an inn and feed, wash and lay ourselves to rest for a good long night."

"But after that?"

He looked toward the sea, then back at her. "I say, fancy a visit to Egypt, love?"

"As long as I'm with you, I'll go anywhere," Eleanor replied. "Because any place where you are is home to me."

And together they looked out to the ever-changing ocean, and wondered where it would take them next.

UNEXPECTED

EVERYTHING COUNTS

UNEXPECTED

EVERYTHING COUNTS

Change was coming. Elspeth Valerin knew it. She'd seen it this morning in her daily calculations. The date, her name and birthday, the color of the sky and what she'd eaten for breakfast—all had been given a numerical value and figured in an equation along with a dozen other factors.

Everything counts, she thought as she followed Gabriana through the carved wooden door to The Slaughtered Lamb. For most people, arithmancy was no more than a jumble of numbers. For Elspeth, it was her life.

"I'm so pleased you decided to come out with us tonight, Elspeth," Gabriana said over her shoulder. "We've been asking you for ages. I thought you'd never say yes."

"The stars must finally have aligned," teased Dayla Mornit. Dayla taught Runes at Somnus Keep.

"No," interjected Callis Dardin. She taught Astronomy. "The numbers finally added up. Am I right, Elspeth?"

Elspeth smiled a bit as she followed her colleagues to a table toward the back of the pub. "Something like that."

The scent of sawdust, alcohol, and food greeted her, and she paused to look around. Seventeen tables, each with three or four chairs. Six windows. A long, polished wood bar stretched along the left side of the room. Twenty-two stools lined up along it. Toward the back, a swinging door leading to the kitchen, and a hallway. A dartboard with eight darts stuck into the cork. Six musicians in the corner struck up a tune to cheers from the substantial crowd.

She was counting again and took a deep breath to force herself to focus on the quality of the pub rather than the quantity of the items within it.

"I admire anyone who can make sense of Arithmancy, much less teach it," said Dayla. "I can't add the contents of my pocket, much less turn everything I do into an equation."

Elspeth gave a tentative smile. "'Tis useful to know how to do it. But 'tis just as useful to know someone who can make the calculations for you."

Dayla stared at her for a moment. "Is it possible our quiet Elspeth has just put me in my place?"

"Oh, no, I—"

"Hush," said Gabriana. "She's teasing you."

Callis laughed, looking at the serving lass headed their way. "Ignore her, Elspeth. She's a sour, old biddy because nobody likes Runes either. And good eve to you, Gretel Deloras!"

Elspeth couldn't help staring at Gretel, whose smile was almost blinding in its brightness. Her lush curves threatened to burst the seams of her simple peasant shirt, worn so low off her shoulders the dusky hint of aureoles peeked out from the lace around the edge. A man's hands would easily span her waist, while her hips swelled out below with the promise of sensual delights any man would be unable to resist.

"Who's your friend?" Gretel's voice oozed such blatant sensuality the men's heads at the next table turned. She leaned forward to smile directly at Elspeth. "Hello, honey. I'm Gretel."

"El...Elspeth," she stammered, overwhelmed by Gretel's presence.

Gretel laughed, tossing back her mane of blonde curls so they fell down her back. "Welcome to The Slaughtered Lamb, sweet thing. What can I get you? We have everything you could want and probably some things you don't."

Elspeth hated the heatroses that bloomed in her cheeks and hoped the pub's dim lighting hid them. At the school she managed to maintain the near-constant cool and collected demeanor necessary to keep her students in line. Here she was out of her element, unused to the attention and uncertain how to react.

Gretel took their orders and glanced again at Elspeth, her bright blue gaze lingering. "Sure I can't bring you something stronger, sweetheart? You're a mite pale. Maybe an ale would do your blood some good."

"All right," she answered, surprising herself. "Ale would be lovely, thank you."

Gretel raised one perfect golden eyebrow, as though Elspeth's politely phrased response had surprised her, but she smiled. "Grand, lass. I'll bring your drinks right over, ladies."

"Sweet Astria, if I looked like her, I'd never get out of bed." Callis shifted in her chair, watching Gretel sashay away.

"You wouldn't?" Elspeth turned to look at the Callis. "Why not? She's beautiful."

Callis looked perplexed for a moment before laughing. "Oh, Elspeth, you're such a dear."

Damn. She'd said the wrong thing. Again. 'Twas a talent, she supposed, to consistently come out with the wrong words.

Gabriana came to her rescue again. "Callis didn't mean she'd stay abed out of grief, Elspeth. She meant that if she looked like Gretel, she'd have so many lovers, she'd never get out of bed."

Again, Elspeth blushed. "Ah. Of course."

In a world where lovemaking was as practiced a pastime as playing a sport or taking up a hobby, the subject of sex was not one that ought to have brought such heat to her cheeks. Yet, of course it did because, though lovemaking was considered not only an enjoyable part of life but a necessary one, Elspeth did not partake.

Her colleagues wouldn't have known that, of course. It wasn't good manners to ask, and she doubted they'd assume she was celibate. She was a magicreator after all. An instructor at Somnus Keep. Arithmancy, the study of numerical values used to make predictions, meant she rarely had to harness the power of the thrall. Nobody had to know her control of it was flawed.

"Here we go, ladies." Gretel returned bearing a tray of glasses she set down in front of all of them with the unerring memory of a good server. "Ale for you, my lovely."

"Thank you."

Gretel smiled and put her hand on her ample hip. "Anything else I can get for you, loves?"

"This will do for now." Dayla sipped from her glass, the foam from the ale coating her upper lip.

Gretel moved away, and Elspeth watched her work the tables. She flirted with the men, and if her obvious pleasure at their attention was false, she did a fine job of making it believable. Envy, fierce and shocking, made Elspeth gulp her ale. A woman with control like that over her body could do anything.

"Two sevendays of freedom!" Gabriana crowed. "What will you do with it?"

Elspeth intended to do the same thing on her holiday she did all the rest of the time—study, read, knit. Perhaps continue to work toward advanced certification in her field.

"Sleep in!" Callis wriggled with a gleeful sound.

"Stay up late," Dayla countered.

"What about you, Elspeth? Have you any grand plans for the holiday?"

She opened her mouth to answer, but before she could, Callis pointed discreetly and gave a whispered giggle. "There he is!"

"Who?" Elspeth asked, even as she followed Callis's pointing finger with her gaze.

"The owner, Conn." Dayla giggled, too. "Isn't he beautiful?"

Conn. The name was not uncommon. Hundreds of mothers must have named their sons the same. The man who owned this pub, the beautiful man who had all the ladies giggling and pointing, did not have to be the same Connell from her past.

But he was.

* * *

"Your admiration club is here," said Gretel as Connell came from the storeroom, hefting a fresh keg to tap.

He settled the keg behind the bar and gave her a grin. "Yeah? Which ones?"

"You're too convinced of your own charm." Gretel rolled her eyes, but nodded toward the back of the room. "The ones from up the hill. From the Keep."

Connell chuckled, bending to drive the spigot into the new keg and sliding an empty glass with practiced ease beneath to catch the spurt of ale. No sense in wasting it, so he swallowed the mouthful and set the empty glass in the bin to be taken back for washing. "The ones who're so free with their coin?"

Gretel poured some shots and set them on her tray. "They brought a new little mouse along with them tonight."

"Yeah?" He stood, wiping his brow on his sleeve.

"Pretty thing with a mouth like sugar."

He laughed. "Yeah?"

Gretel nodded. "Shy, though. I thought she was going to burst into flame when I asked her name."

He rolled his head on his shoulders, cracking his neck and shaking out the tension. "Not everyone can flirt with you, love."

Gretel smiled. "That's what you think, Conn-me-love."

He laughed as she swished her hips and headed back to serving. He looked out over the room, eyes taking in everything. Connell Byrne prided himself on running the finest pub in town. The Slaughtered Lamb was a clean joint, with the best food and beverage he could provide, the fastest service, the liveliest entertainment. He didn't allow dirty dealings in the Lamb either, and if that meant cracking a few skulls to keep out the riff raff...well, he wasn't above it. Bar fights were part of the business, but as he scanned the crowd, he saw no sign of belligerence waiting to erupt into violence.

The trill of feminine laughter from the back of the room caught his ear, and grinning, he turned to look. Gretel was right in saying he knew too well his own charm. The ladies came in to eat, drink and be merry, and if a little harmless flirting made them merry, Connell wasn't above that either.

He recognized the group as one that had been in before. They were all magicreators from up the hill. Instructors at the Keep, which meant they always had plenty of coin to spread around. That suited him fine. Magicreators didn't cause trouble either, because even a group of unattended women wouldn't be bothered by the most boisterous of his customers. No man would mess with a magicreator who could take off his nuts with little more than a flick of her fingers.

Connell walked around the edge of the bar and headed toward their table, intending to give them a smile and a laugh, and a round of free drinks in appreciation of their business. Maybe let them think they might have the chance to take him to bed. It never hurt to lead them on. Made them spendy, it did.

"Good evening, ladies," he said, hands on his hips, looking round at each of them. "A pleasure to see—"

The words caught in his throat at the sight of her. The same dark hair, worn tied up instead of loose but still as smooth as silk. Time had sharpened her features and turned her from a girl into a woman, but the better-defined cheekbones and jaw only made her that much more beautiful. The lush lips he'd once kissed with such passion parted as he spoke, and the remembered taste of her set his mind reeling.

"Hello, Connell." This came from the red-haired woman to his left. She eyed him without a speck of coyness. "Nice to see you again."

"And you," he answered, eyes locked on Ella's familiar, blue-gray gaze. The eyes he'd never thought to see again.

The other women didn't seem to notice his lack of attention for they giggled and flirted while his mouth made replies his mind did not bother to track.

She was terrified. He could see it in the way her eyes grew dark and her fingers tightened on her glass. Her entire body vibrated like she meant to run away, but was unable to move.

He scared her, 'twas no great feat to see it, and, even after all this time, the fact she would fear him tightened his jaw with anger. He'd never done aught to harm her. All he'd ever done was love her. And even now, ten years after he'd told her he would never love another woman the way he loved her, she wanted to run away from him again.

"…on the house," he heard himself say, and waved away the ladies' half-hearted protests. "I insist. On me."

"Ooh," purred the woman with black hair. "Really? Drinks on you? That would be interesting."

Where he'd have given her a grin and a wink before, now Connell only managed a faint smile. "Be careful, madam, or I'll think you fancy me."

This made the women at the table erupt into giddy laughter. All but one. He stared hard into her eyes for one more moment before turning away.

* * *

Three ales. She'd kept careful count, as she did of everything, even now when the alcohol fuzzed her brain and made her unsteady.

The others had become raucous as the night wore on, setting up challenges with the table of men beside them. Drinking games. Wagers. Callis had settled herself upon the lap of a brawny man with a ginger-colored beard and a booming laugh. Dayla and Gabriana had agreed to a game of darts with two men, though their opponents had declared the match unfair because the women could use magic to their advantage.

Everything in pairs, Elspeth thought as she stared at the bottom of another empty glass. *Two by two. Neat and tidy. No room for three.* She was drunk, which surprised her into laughter. She put her hand over her mouth to stifle it, though nobody would have noticed with all the noise.

"What's with your friend?" she heard the brawny man ask Callis. "She don't like comp'ny?"

Callis murmured something Elspeth couldn't hear, and she stared at the table. Men had been speaking to her all night, but she'd put them all off. The only man for whom she had eyes had not looked at her again, a fact for which she was intensely grateful as his studied lack of attention allowed her to watch him, unnoticed.

Connell. Ten years had been kind to him. They'd broadened his shoulders, lengthened his hair, and touched the corners of his eyes with lines that showed he, at least, had spent his time smiling. He wasn't a lad any longer, but a man, but then again she supposed she could no longer consider herself a girl.

She was no fool. She was an Arithmanticist. Elspeth knew better than anyone how small choices influence greater ones, and how one seemingly unimportant decision can affect an entire outcome. Everything counts.

If she was here, and Connell, too, it meant that somehow along the way both of them had done something, made some choice, taken some branching path that led them both to this spot. It would not have happened otherwise. She would have refused the invitation to join her colleagues, or they'd have taken her to another pub. Or going further back, he'd not have opened his place in this town where she'd chosen to live.

She was here, and he was here, and there was a purpose to it. A fate she could not comprehend. An equation she did not know how to calculate.

All at once the drinks, the smoke and the laughter made her blink against an onslaught of dizziness. She stood, touching one hand to the table to steady herself.

"I'm going to get some fresh air," she told Callis.

"Are you well?" Callis looked concerned, as though she meant to get up from her companion's lap.

"I'm fine," Elspeth answered quickly, adding a smile to be more convincing. "Just need a bit of a breeze. That's all."

Callis nodded, but sank back onto her seat. "If you're sure…"

"Yes. I'm sure." Elspeth smiled again and moved around the table, avoiding the leer and lewd greeting of one of the men sitting there.

Darkness shrouded the hallway leading to the washrooms, but Elspeth had never feared darkness. She went past two doors marked with symbols—one for male and one for female. Again, a pair. The door at the hall's end bore no marking, but she knew it led outside, and so she pushed through it and ventured into the chill winter air.

The fenced courtyard behind the Lamb contained no pretty garden or bubbling fountain, only a path of fitted slates leading to a leaning, decrepit shed and scrubby grass interspersed with patches of bare earth. Large refuse bins lined one side. Some benches lined another, and 'twas there she sought to rest her legs and catch the breath which had left her with such sudden ferocity inside.

Above her, the stars gleamed pure white against a black, clear sky. The moon hung like a coin amongst them. She smelled snow despite the lack of clouds. She tipped her head to stare up, and her eyes followed the lines and curves of the constellations as she began to count the points of light.

She'd never counted them all. She never could. It brought her peace, though, to try. Stars were just about the only limitless thing in the world, the only things she could not reach the end of, and the numbers rose higher and higher in her mind, wiping out everything else for the moment.

A star has fallen to earth. The next moment proved her wrong. Not a star. An ember. A cheroot, the tip flaring as its owner drew in the smoke, then arcing through the air as he tossed it to the ground and left it without bothering to crush it with his boot. A smaller piece of blackness separated from the larger shadows, and she stood, stepping back against the fence.

"How many are there?"

She'd known 'twas him the moment she stood. "You know I can't know that."

"Not even you? Not the Countess?"

"Don't call me that." The retort came out sharper than she'd intended. The fence pressed against her back. A splinter gouged her arm. She'd come out without a cloak.

Connell stepped closer. "You used to like it when I called you that."

"That was a long time ago." Elspeth couldn't back away any further, so she straightened her spine. *And you used to say it with love in your voice.*

Connell's eyes flashed in the starlight, and a moment later, his teeth as he grinned. "Aye, and so it was. A long time ago and a place far away. But you haven't changed, have you? You're still counting."

He'd moved so close to her she could smell him, and it made her weak. He'd used to smell of the sea. Salt. Sun. Sand. The tang of sweat.

Now he smelled of ale and smoke, but underlying it still a hint of sun and wind and sand. He was different and yet the same; the remembered taste of him flooded her mouth and made her heart thump in her chest.

"I'm still counting." Her voice scratched and cracked, embarrassed her.

His hand came out to twirl a strand of hair that had fallen over her shoulder. A handspan separated them, no more. He tucked the hair behind her ear. His fingers cupped her cheek, then trailed along her jaw, down the line of her neck and came to rest upon her shoulder.

She shivered, not from cold, but from the heat that had sprung up along the path of his fingers. Shadows veiled his face again, but she heard his breath, felt it on her face, and she could almost taste his lips on hers.

Connell didn't kiss her. "I didn't believe my eyes when I saw you sitting in my pub. After all this time and there you were, looking like an angel. I thought for sure I was dreaming."

She wanted to tell him she was sorry. She hadn't meant to run away. She hadn't meant to hurt him. She hadn't meant any of it, that long ago night when she'd told him she could never love him...but unlike numbers, words never came to her rescue when she needed them.

Closer still he moved, his body against hers, pinning her against the fence and Elspeth shuddered with a sudden force of desire so strong it forced a low cry from her throat. Ten years, and he still affected her this way. The only man who ever could.

She was already opening her mouth to his kiss when he pulled away, leaving her cold instead of hot. Connell backed away with a muttered curse. She blinked, trying to see his expression, but could make out nothing more than the flash of his eyes again in starlight.

"Why?" he asked her, one word that meant so much and had so many answers.

She didn't know which to give him. "Connell..."

He backed away from her reaching hand, putting both his own up as though to make sure there was no way they could possibly touch her.

"Why, Ella?" The agony in his voice broke her heart all over again. "Why now, after all this time, when I finally thought—"

But he'd say no more, just backed away another step. This time, she was the one pursuing, moving across the slate path toward him. "Connell, wait."

"You're still afraid of me!" he cried. "I saw it inside, and I felt you shaking just now! You're afraid of me, even now, when I'd never do aught to hurt you!"

"I know that. I know it. Connell, love, please…"

He'd backed into a patch of moonlight, and to her horror, she saw tears glimmering in his eyes. She'd made him cry before, and it seemed unfair now that she'd made him weep again when tears would never come for her no matter how much she might wish for the relief they brought.

He ran a hand through his hair, messing it, and let his hand rest on the back of his neck, his eyes turned away from her. "Why?"

"Because I was a fool," she answered. "I didn't deserve you."

She reached for him again, a hesitant hand that did not quite touch him. "I was a fool who did not know the gift she held, Connell. And I plead your mercy."

He shook his head. "You left without a word. I never knew where you'd gone, or if you were all right. I never knew if you were alive or dead, sick or well. I never knew if you were happy."

"I'm sorry." 'Twas all she had to say, and 'twas not enough.

"All I ever did was love you," he said in a low voice. "And you treated me like I wasn't even worth it."

Then she was in his arms and his mouth was on hers, bruising. She didn't resist, didn't protest, just let him walk her backward and put her up against the fence, his hands on her waist and his mouth crushing, crushing.

She opened beneath him and his tongue swept inside. She tasted ale and smoke. She tasted Connell, a flavor she'd never forgotten, and it made her gasp as she put her arms around his neck and clung to him.

He pushed hard against her, the way he used to when they were in her garden and desperate to steal one more kiss before she had to go inside. He bunched the fabric of her skirt in his hands and slid beneath it to the bare skin of her thighs atop her stockings. His hands cupped her rear and he lifted her, holding her so tight she had no fear of falling. The heat and hardness of him pressed against her, and she gasped and tightened her thighs around his hips.

She tasted blood from the force of his kiss, from a spot where her teeth had caught the inside of her lip. The metallic, salty taste of it made her think of the way they'd been, and how she'd once taken him in her mouth while the ocean crashed so close to them the spray had wet their clothes.

Desire, unaccustomed and overwhelming, flooded her, but she didn't fight it. Her arms tightened on his neck and she kissed him as fiercely as he did her, their mouths meeting again and again, reminding her of the way eagles mated in the sky, soaring and plummeting as they screeched their pleasure.

He held her against the splintered wood with one hand while the other slid between them to fumble with the laces at his waistband. His hand rubbed her through the thin material of her undergarment, and she shuddered with want.

He'd be inside her in another moment, and oh, by the Astria, she wanted him there. Inside her. Filling her. Making this feeling grow until she exploded the way she used to when they were young, before it had all gone so wrong.

He shifted her weight and she tensed, waiting for him to enter her. Then, in the next moment, she stood on her own, her skirt falling down around her ankles and the fence the only thing holding her up. She blinked, bereft and abandoned, her body not yet adjusted to the loss of his hands on her. She licked her lips and tasted more blood, and she lifted a shaking hand to wipe them clean.

"You might not have changed," he said in a shaking voice. "But I have. I'll not be used like that again, no matter what treasure you hold between your legs."

His words hurt, that he thought she'd ever used him. He twisted away from her when she tried to touch his cheek, and she let her hand fall. He ran his hand again through his hair, then crossed his arms over his chest. The white moonlight made stark lines on his face, cast his eyes into shadow and highlighted his scowl.

"All these years," he told her. "You've no right to come here, to my place, looking as though naught's changed. No right."

His words were unfair, but she accepted them with a nod. "I'll go then, shall I?"

"Aye, go." He bit out the words like they tasted bad. "Get out of my place, and don't come back here."

She didn't move. They stared at each other until at last she nodded again. "I plead your mercy, Connell. I never meant to hurt you."

"No." His reply was colder than the winter air. "And I can see by your tears how grieved you are."

His short, sharp burst of laughter pierced her heart.

"Ah, but then, you've never wept, have you? Why should I expect you'd bother to cry for me?"

"If I could have, believe me, I would."

He didn't answer. She backed away from him, turned and left the courtyard, wishing desperately she could have given him tears but as always, finding none to give.

* * *

She came to him in dreams, as she always did. The girl he'd loved so much it had been like dying when she left him. Tonight she was the woman she'd become, the one he did not know.

The taste of her had changed, as had the curve of her hips, the fullness of her breasts, the timbre of her voice. He took her in his arms and she yielded, offering her mouth to his kiss and her body to his hands.

He took her without a word, as once they'd not needed to speak. She opened beneath him. His tongue stroked hers. His hands roamed her body. She linked her arms behind his neck, and he lifted her, laying her down upon a bed of flowers that filled the air with their scent as the weight of their bodies crushed the petals.

His mouth traced the line of her chin and the slope of her throat. Her pulse beat under his lips and he licked the spot. Ella arched beneath him, murmuring the name only she had ever called him. To everyone else he was Conn. To her, he'd always been Connell, and she always made it sound noble.

"The name of a prince."

Her smile made his heart thump inside his chest and he kissed her again, covering her with his body, the body of the man he was now and not the lad he'd been.

"I'm no prince."

"You have ever been my prince." Her eyes shone. "Ever and always."

And the thing of it was, with her he had always felt a prince, rather than the beggar he really was. A nobleman, not the son of a butler and a cook. Ella made him feel as though he could be and do anything, that he needn't contort himself into the place his parents had expected him to take.

"Everything I've become is because of you," he told her.

Her hands linked around the back of his neck, pulling him down to her mouth again, and he kissed her like 'twas the last thing he'd ever do on this earth.

His hand slid up to cup her breast through the thin flaxene of her gown, and he passed a thumb over her nipple. In another moment, he slid down to take it in his mouth through the cloth, and in the next, the dream shifted and they were both naked on the bed of flowers which he knew from real life to be somewhat scratchy but here, in the dream realm, were as soft as feather bed.

She tasted of sunshine, his Ella did. His mouth moved along her body, along the soft curve of her belly, the slope of her hip, the warm skin of her thighs. He found her center. The sound of her low cry when he kissed her there made his cock twitch in response. He licked her, and she arched upward. Her fingers tightened in his hair. He found the small button of her pleasure and stroked it with his tongue until she gasped his name over and over again.

He had always loved making her shudder beneath him. He loved the taste of her desire, and the way her smooth folds swelled as she grew hot with passion. He loved the way her clit grew stiff between his lips, and the way it throbbed when she came.

"I love you," he said into her ear as once again he stretched his body along hers. "I'll never love any woman the way I love you."

And because this was a dream, thank the Astria, she did not turn him away but looked into his eyes and put her arms around him, and she took him inside her body.

"I love you, too, Connell," his dream-Ella told him as urged him to move with an upward shift of her hips. She said the words she'd said to him once before, long ago and far away, before it had all disintegrated around them. "Make love to me."

Long ago and far away, he had not been able to do as she'd asked. He'd made love to dozens of women since that night. Fair-haired and dark, with eyes of blue and green and brown and gray, with bodies of every shape and voices in every tone. Every one of them became Ella at the moment of his climax.

But now, in this moment, as he moved within her, it really was Ella and he didn't have to pretend. He kissed her, the taste of her spurring him on. Her nails raked down his back and he moaned, though the pain only enhanced his pleasure. He moved faster.

"I love you," she said, her blue-gray eyes never leaving his. "I always have. And I always will."

Ecstasy boiled inside him, making him shake, and he wanted to bury his face in her hair, but couldn't pull himself from the sight of her eyes. He moved inside her heat, watching desire make her tilt her head on its pillow of lilies. Her gaze never left his, and he drowned in those eyes, the color of the sea on a cloudy day, her eyes that never wept, and he saw himself reflected there as he climaxed.

And woke, sweating, the sheets a tangled mess around his ankles and his cock throbbing with a need for release so great it made his stomach hurt. Connell sat up and scrubbed his face with his palms, breathing hard. A dream was all it had been, but he mourned the loss of it anyway, because dreams were all he had of her.

He swung his legs over the side of the bed and went into his washroom, seeking the solace of a cold shower, the only relief he'd have that night. As he closed his eyes against the needling spray, he saw her face, and he whispered her name, letting his mouth fill with water that couldn't wash away the memory of her flavor.

* * *

"Mistress Valerin, sit." Riordan de Cimmerian, Instructor Primus of Magical Theory and Practice, indicated the chair in front of his desk.

Elspeth sat. She slid a sheaf of parchment across his desk. "I've completed the requirements for the Consummo degree, sir. I would request you review the work and approve it before I send it to the Arithmancy Accreditation Committee."

He nodded and pushed the papers to one side. "Quite a lot of work for you to be doing during the winter break. You're entitled to some time away from your job, Mistress Valerin."

She gave a small smile. "As are you, sir, and yet here I find you at your desk."

The Instructor Primus had a reputation for being a man quick to anger and swift to disdain, and though Elspeth had seen him behave that way with many others, with her he seemed more often to maintain an air of quiet bemusement or consideration. What, exactly, he was considering about her she never dared ponder. She didn't wish to know. 'Twas enough for her that he had hired her knowing her control of the thrall was flawed, and that he never asked her of her past. He'd earned her loyalty for that alone, and Elspeth's loyalty, once earned, was fierce and unrelenting.

"Mistress Valerin," de Cimmerian now said, "I must speak with you on a matter of some import."

"Sir?" Her stomach twisted. His dark eyes traveled over her face, and he had that look again. As though she were a puzzle he meant to decipher.

"You have been a teacher here for seven years."

"Yes, sir."

"And in all that time, it has never come to my attention that you've taken a lover."

For a moment she didn't know quite what to say. Her mouth parted in surprise before she closed it. Those words were the last she'd ever have expected from him.

"Sir, I fail to see—"

His raised hand stopped her. "In all that time, I have watched you teach your craft to class after class. You are one of my finest instructors. You have an easy way about you that makes Arithmancy appeal to even those who find numbers appallingly difficult. You care for your students. I know you have open office hours longer than any of your colleagues, and I know as well the number of students you counsel."

"They come to me because I listen to them," she said.

"Because once you needed someone to listen to you and had nobody."

His assessment of her made her body stiffen so suddenly she pushed the chair back from the desk. "Sir—"

Again, he raised his hand and she fell silent. "I've watched you teach, Mistress Valerin, and I've seen you are capable of passion. So tell me, please, why you can express it with equations and calculations, but not with a lover?"

She wanted to run, but could not. His dark eyes pinned her in place. She shook her head slightly and had to wet her lips, but still could not speak.

"Who hurt you so badly you can't open yourself?"

She had seen him be cold to others and had seen his sneer. This was worse, this penetrating insistence upon truth. Nobody else seemed to notice or care about what was inside her, but this man did. She couldn't hide from him. He was the most powerful magicreator in the Keep, the strongest she'd ever known.

"I have never asked you why your control of the thrall is incomplete," he told her, his voice gentler than she'd have expected from him. "But I don't have to ask to know. I've seen it before. Rarely, thank the Astria, for it rarely happens. But I do know."

Her throat closed. Another woman would have cried, but again the release of tears was denied her. She ducked her head, eyes fixed upon her hands fisted in her lap. "I have worked hard, sir, to gain better control of it. I am much improved."

"You shouldn't have had to work so hard."

The anger in his voice made her look up, but he was not angry with her. He was angry *for* her, and Elspeth understood something about him few probably did, for he hid his heart beneath an exterior of disdain, as she did behind a mask of dispassion. Riordan de Cimmerian cared deeply about his students and his staff. He cared about her.

"Who was he?" he asked her. "The one who took from you instead of giving. Tell me, and I'll see he's punished for it, no matter where he is."

"He is dead," she said. "And beyond punishment. He slit his wrists and bled to death in our mother's rose garden. I was ten-and-eight."

The implications of what she'd revealed hung between them. She met his gaze and didn't look away.

"Then you've never had an *ahavatara*," he said quietly. "No first true lover whose duty it is to open your body to love and your soul to the glory of the thrall. You were forced."

She nodded. She had never spoken to anyone of the things Des had done to her. Never admitted her shame. Not since the day in her mother's garden when she'd lied and told Connell she didn't and would never love him.

"Elspeth, you are not to blame."

She nodded again. "I know."

"But you don't believe."

She gave a small shake of her head, a shrug. "'Twas a long time ago."

De Cimmerian stared at her for a long, silent moment. He sighed, and again she caught a glimpse of the man he hid from everyone else. "'Tis not my place to tell you that you must take a lover. I do well understand your reluctance to do so. But you do understand that the damage he did you need not be permanent, do you not? You need not forever mishandle your magic because of one man's disservice?"

She nodded slowly. "I do so understand, sir. I do."

"Come here." He stood, and she obeyed, her heart hammering.

He waited until she stood in front of him. He was a tall man, and he put a finger beneath her chin to lift it. He bent to kiss her, his lips pausing before they touched hers. "You trust me, don't you?"

"I do, sir."

"And yet you are shaking, and not from desire."

She looked into his eyes. "I plead your mercy."

He ran a hand along her neck, down her shoulder, brushing the hair off it. Then he stepped back. "You need plead nothing from me, Elspeth. I would not force attentions upon you. I understand why you shield yourself."

Looking into his eyes, she thought he did. Riordan de Cimmerian had his own demons, his own reasons for keeping his heart as closed as hers. That he had been willing to help her meant all the more.

She thought of Connell. The courtyard. His bruising kiss and the inside of her lip still wounded from it.

She looked at de Cimmerian. "I made a mistake ten years ago, and threw away the love of a man who would have given me everything."

"A magicreator?"

She shook her head. "He was the son of my parents' butler and cook. We had known each other since infancy. We played together as children. And when we got older..." She smiled a little. "We were foolish. We thought nobody would know."

"But you could not take him as your *ahavatara* because he did not have magic."

Again, she nodded. "Yes."

"Did he know what happened to you?"

She hesitated, remembering. "Yes. He knew. He blamed himself for not protecting me. But when he tried to love me, I couldn't let him. I ran away."

"And now?"

"Now," she said slowly, "I have found him again."

"Then might I suggest, Mistress Valerin, you don't let your opportunity slide away again?"

Once again he was the Instructor Primus, distant, though now his consideration of her had disappeared. *Because he knew,* she thought. She was no longer a mystery to him. He understood her now, and he did not despise her for her past.

She'd experienced moments of revelation in her work when the columns of figures had formed a picture so clear and precise 'twas impossible to ignore. Now, even without the equations, she understood something so clear and shining she felt the worst sort of fool for being blind to it before.

Riordan de Cimmerian, a man neither kind nor generous by any description, knew her truth, and he did not hate her for it. He did not turn from her in disgust, and he did not even love her.

If a man who did not love her did not turn from her in disgust, neither would a man who did.

"I understand, sir. And, sir, if I might be so bold..." She paused. "You might take your own advice."

His eyes narrowed, and again she caught the glimpse of the man who so many feared. "You are bold."

She nodded. "I plead your mercy."

He stared at her a moment longer, the weight of his gaze unreadable. "You're dismissed, Mistress Valerin."

"Thank you, sir."

He nodded, not looking at her any more. Elspeth left his office with much to think about.

Arithmancy was a far more precise practice than Divination. Divination used signs and portents to predict the future, while Arithmancy used numbers and calculations to determine how choices would affect outcomes. The difference of something as simple as one number could result in an end completely different than if one used another number or calculation to figure it.

She spent several hours at her desk, running numbers. She factored every possible equation, ran every scenario she could think of, added and subtracted every element. It was, perhaps, the mathematical equivalent of "he loves me, he loves me not," but it was what she knew best how to do. In the end, it came down to two results, the difference of one small equation, one factor, a single number that when used or eliminated in the overall formula created two results. One, positive. The other, negative.

When it came down to the line, there was nothing she could do to determine which of the sums was going to be accurate. No choice she could make to sway the results. Two outcomes seemed equally likely.

She couldn't put a numerical value on love; couldn't use addition and subtraction on the human heart. It didn't work. She could fact and figure her way into an assumption of the future, and use the numbers to lead her choices toward positive or negative, but in the end, it all came down to something she could not control.

Either Connell loved her, or he did not. And no matter how many times she looked at the numbers, she wasn't able to decide which of the two most likely results were going to happen.

*   *   *

"Connell."

His eyes opened wide to darkness and he sat up. The curtains blew in the open window. The chill, salt-scented breeze made him shiver.

"Ella?"

A portion of the darkness peeled away from the doorframe. In the next moment she slid under the covers and into his arms. His nose filled with her scent, while the dark silk of her hair tickled his bare chest. She wore a thin flaxene gown, and his hands told him she was bare beneath it. The points of her nipples rose hard against the cloth, and at the feeling of them, he was hard, too.

"Make love to me, Connell."

Oh, how badly he wanted to. Her mouth was already on his, her tongue darting between his lips with the delicate aggressiveness that never failed to stiffen his cock and make his heart pound. His hands tangled in her the glory of her hair, and she moaned when he tugged it. She moaned louder when his teeth found the soft flesh of her throat.

He had no fear they'd be overheard. His secluded rooms over the garden shed meant only someone standing down there in the night, listening on purpose, could possibly hear her. Yet something made him hush her. He put her from him a little more roughly than he'd intended, and the whimper as his fingers gripped her arms made his heart lurch with grief.

"Ella," he said. "I want to make love to you. But we can't."

She sat up. Moonlight filtered through the window and flashed in her eyes. She was crying. "We have to."

Connell shook his head, pushing her hair away from her beautiful face, and knew he was dreaming this as he'd dreamed so many other times because he already knew her reasons for seeking the safety of his bed when they both had always known he could not be her first lover.

He could not be her *ahavatara*. He didn't have magic. Giving him her virginity meant she'd tithe herself to him forever, her use of the thrall would be compromised, and she would never reach her full potential as a magicreator. They'd always known it. They'd always known their desire needed limits. One day she would no longer be his Ella but belong to someone else.

"I don't care," she whispered. "I love you, Connell. You. And I want to be with you. I don't care if I never harness the thrall, I don't care—"

She did care. He knew that. She had to. She had no choice. Elspeth had magic, and it couldn't be denied. He had nothing but a strong back and hands that could build. Nothing but sweat and effort. She had the chance to have it all, but not if she wasted it on him.

"Ella, I can't let you—"

"Please, Connell!" Tears choked her voice, and she shook in his arms. "Please, before it's too late! Once 'tis done, he'll be able to do naught about it—"

"Who, Ella? Who?"

Silver tears slipped down her cheeks, like trails of star fire. "He said he'd make sure Mother and Father put you out…and your parents, too. And that he'd kill you himself, if he knew you'd laid a hand on me again. He said I'm bringing shame to our family, that I'd better not disgrace him by tithing myself to someone with no magic!"

"Your brother doesn't scare me," Connell said angrily, but the sight of her face made him fall silent.

For the first time, he saw why his Ella had gone so pale and thin the past few months. Why she'd stopped smiling. His fingers tightened further, and her small cry made him relax. His heart had lodged in his throat. "I'll tear him apart."

"I'll give it all up. I don't care." She sounded hoarse, her voice like glass, brittle. Ready to shatter. "Make love to me, Connell, and all I'll lose is the thrall. I can live with the rest of my life doing only low magic. I can. But I can't live the rest of my life tithed to him. I can't! Not that way!"

He hushed her, gathering her into his arms, burying his face in her hair. He didn't want to ask her what Des had done or what he was trying to do. He didn't want to believe it. His stomach twisted, but the words she'd said no longer mattered. She was with him now. His Ella, the only woman he would ever love.

And then, another figure appeared in the doorway. The shouting began. Desmond Valerin, his parents' pride and joy, and supposed defender of his sister's virtue. He'd cried of scandal and threatened to kill Connell, and because Desmond was a magicreator and Connell not, the fight had been brief and unfair. By the time the binding spell wore off and Connell could leave his room, much had happened. The rose garden had been painted with Des's blood.

And Ella had been lost.

"Connell."

His eyes opened wide to darkness, and he sat up. He was no longer dreaming. A shadow in his doorway had him on his feet in moments, fists raised.

She murmured a word and the fire flared. She pushed her hair off her shoulders and looked at him, her eyes glimmering in the light. "I didn't mean to scare you."

"You didn't." He ran a hand through his hair, then looked down, self-conscious at his bare chest and the loosely tied sleeping trousers he wore. "What are you doing here?"

Ella –Elspeth, he corrected himself, looked hesitant. "I came to plead your mercy. For everything. All of it. I have no excuses. I was cruel then. You deserved better."

This wasn't what he'd expected, and though her words softened him inside, he did his best not to show it. "You have my mercy. Now you can go."

She did something he had not expected. She crossed the room and went to her knees in front of him, head bowed. "Connell, please, please forgive me."

And he could no longer hold his anger. It had burned through him like a hot coal in a napkin, leaving behind a hole, but no more heat. He got down in front of her, unable to bear seeing her abase herself like that. "I forgive you, Ella. I told you that."

She looked up at him. "Do you still hate me?"

"I could never hate you."

Her smile was small. "You told me you hated me."

"You told me you'd never love me."

"I didn't want to hurt you." She looked at him. "Des was dead by his own hand. My mother—"

"I remember."

Her mother had given her favored child a funeral full of pomp and circumstance, of glitter and glory. Amarata Valerin had slapped her daughter's face in front of the mourners, called her a whore and blamed her for Desmond's death.

"When you found me in the garden afterward and took my hand, all I could do was think how my mother was right." She took a deep breath and reached for his hand. She linked their fingers together. "How it was my fault Des had died. And how I couldn't let her know how much I loved you, Connell, or else she'd send you away or find a way to hurt you out of spite for me. So I told you I didn't love you, and I pushed you away because I didn't know what else to do, and I went away because I couldn't bear to live with how much I'd hurt you."

He pulled her into his arms. "You weren't crying. I thought you meant it. I shouldn't have believed it, Ella. I should've known different."

Against his cheek, she shook her head. "You couldn't have."

He held her tight against him, stroking her hair and losing himself in her scent the way he'd done so many years ago, when they were no longer children and not quite adults. Tears wet his face, and he wasn't sure if they belonged to her or to him, only that she was laughing and crying at the same time, and then she was kissing him.

"Make love to me," his Ella said to him once again, after all this time. "Please, Connell."

And this time there was no hesitation, no reason to say no. This time, he took her in his arms and carried her to his bed where they fell, both of them laughing until the laughter became sighs.

* * *

He laid her down and covered her with his body. His hands came up to cup the sides of her face and brush the hair away. He looked into her eyes. Then he kissed her with such gentleness it made her want to weep again.

She gave him the tears she'd been unable to shed for years, and he kissed them away. He kissed her eyes, her cheek, the line of her jaw. Connell nuzzled her ear, then the curve of her shoulder, and she tipped her head back to give him access to her throat, and he kissed her there, too.

His mouth, wet heat, with a hint of teeth, made her gasp. He took her skin in his teeth and she arched into his bite. His hands moved down along her sides, then up to cup her breasts through her gown. She moaned his name.

"Ella," he whispered, "I never stopped loving you. Not ever."

"I never stopped loving you either."

He paused in kissing her to prop himself on his elbows and look into her eyes. "I should've protected you."

"Shhh." She shook her head. "That's all gone. He's gone. It's in the past. Let's make the present, here. Now."

She reached up to pull him down to her. Their mouths met, opened, tongues darting, and it was as though no time had ever passed between them. He set her on fire as he always had. As no other man ever had. She took his hand and brought it again to her breast.

He shivered and bent back to her neck, kissing and nibbling. She arched into his touch, encouraging him with small moans. He knew already how to touch her, how to urge her passion from her, only now each touch, each lick, each stroke and nibble, was magnified because it had been so long for her without pleasure, without passion, so long without the ability to feel.

He moved down, undoing the small pearl buttons that lined her dress from throat to hem. Connell laid open the throat of her gown, baring her skin to his kiss. He found the curve of her collarbone and nipped it, earning a gasp, then smoothed his tongue along the place his teeth had already found. He kissed further down, his hands undoing the buttons without hesitation.

He undid the buttons to her waist. Under her gown she wore a thin flaxene shift tied at the throat with ribbons. Connell unlaced her slowly while he kissed her mouth. The heat of his hands on her bare skin made her gasp.

"Your skin is like silk," he whispered.

His fingers circled her nipples, already hard, and he rolled them in the way he used to. The way that made tingling sparks of pleasure flood her veins, move along her body with each beat of her heart. Something had happened to her that made her gasp at the realization.

"I've stopped," she said.

He looked at her. "Stopped what, love?"

"Counting," she said, and kissed him again.

He left her mouth and moved downward again, lips sliding over her skin until he replaced his fingers with his tongue upon her nipples. He suckled first one, then the other, and she shivered under his touch. His hands slid down along the curve of her hips. His mouth kissed her ribs, then the hollow of her naval and the slight curve of her belly. He licked and kissed and nuzzled her skin.

He paused to take her hand and pull her up so she could slip her arms out of her clothes. Sitting, she bared herself to him, nervous for the first time. She was no longer the girl he'd loved. Time had been kind to her, but her body had changed. She pushed the material down over her hips and watched him watch her, his dark eyes gone darker with passion.

"By the Astria, you are beautiful."

Other men had told her so. Ones she'd ignored or avoided. Being told of her beauty had always made her stomach twist, made her turn away. Made her go cold inside.

Not with Connell. His words made her smile. Heat bloomed inside her, sending a flush along her chest and up her throat to paint her cheeks. She wriggled the rest of the way out of her gown and lay back against the headboard, holding out her arms to him.

He stretched out along her once more. They kissed. Long ago they'd spent hours kissing, tongues stroking, lips nibbling. Hands touching first over clothes and then, when it became too much to bear, fingers sliding beneath to pet and rub. And finally, clothes removed, mouths and hands arousing each other, doing everything but the one thing they couldn't do because it would change their lives forever.

His erection rubbed against her through his sleeping trousers, and Elspeth reached down to stroke him. Connell, face buried in her neck, shuddered when she touched him. His teeth closed her skin, giving her the pleasure-pain she'd always loved.

She let her hand move up and down, then reached for the ties at his waistband. "I would see you."

He nodded and helped her undress him as he'd helped her. In moments he was bare, and she put her hand upon his shoulder to push him back against the pillows. She wanted to see all of him. She wanted to drink the sight of him like she'd drink fine wine, wanted to consume him with her eyes.

His body had changed, too. He'd always been strongly built, with muscled arms, broad shoulders, lean hips and strong legs. As a lad of ten-and-eight, dark curling hair had thatched the base of his penis and run in a line up his belly. Now, as a man of eight-and-twenty, the line had thickened. More curling hair scattered over his smooth skin and surrounded the dark circles of his nipples.

She bent to lick one, then the other. He tasted spicy. She sucked his skin gently, hair tickling her cheek, then let her mouth linger on his skin. Warm. Smooth. The same, but different. His body had grown more defined with age. A rippled scar curved along one shoulder.

She moved to kiss his mouth again, her hands running down his arms to circle his wrists, and she pulled away to turn over his hands. The palms were rough. Scars dotted his skin there too. Marks of hard work. She traced them with her fingertips first, then her kisses, and held them up.

"Each of these must tell a story."

He nodded, drawing her closer to kiss her. "For another time."

She laughed as he put his arms around her to hold her close. Their bodies, length to length, skin warm, fit together like puzzle pieces. She took his kiss and gave it back.

"Another time, oh and aye," she agreed.

Her hand found his cock again, and she stroked him gently, fingers barely grasping him. She let her palm roll over the head, then twist around and down the shaft. Up again, the rhythm familiar even after so long.

He sighed into her mouth. She took his breath. He entered her lungs. Became part of her. His hand found the back of her head and held her mouth against him as his hips lifted into her touch.

She broke the kiss to catch her breath. She shifted her legs, and the sensation made her shiver. Heat filled the pit of her belly and lower. She felt swollen, slick with arousal, empty and yearning to be filled.

The first time she'd taken him in her mouth, he'd cried out her name so loud it had startled a colony of gulls. She'd been clumsy then, her love for him making up for her lack of skill, and it had taken only moments for him to spill inside her mouth. Time had granted both of them greater control. The memory of it, the musky, ocean taste of him, made her clit pulse.

Elspeth slid down his body, her mouth leaving a trail of slickness along his skin. She let her breath caress his length, her lips hovering, but not touching him. She heard him take in a breath, but did not hear him let it out, and she smiled. She licked the head of his cock. Connell moaned.

She could not torture him longer, or herself. She wanted to taste him. Elspeth took him into her mouth, the entire length as far as she could. The brush of his pubic hair tickled her lips. He cried her name, and though there were no gulls to scatter above them, the sound of it well-pleased her.

She slid her mouth upward, following behind it with her hand so he was not left bereft. She suckled the head of his cock in time to her hand's stroking. Then down again, slowly, deliberately, until again her mouth brushed his dark hair and her hand slipped down to cup the weight of his balls.

She had always loved doing this for him, giving him pure pleasure. Letting him fill her mouth gave her almost as much pleasure as him filling her, because she loved him.

"Ella." His voice hoarse, Connell moved his hips in time to the pace she'd set. His fingers tangled in her hair, not forcing her to stay there, but moving with her as she moved.

He grew harder under her tongue. His breathing got faster. Between his legs his heartbeat quickened when she pressed the seam of his skin below his testicles. He moaned louder when she ran her finger along that soft skin and pressed in time to her sucking.

A drop of salty fluid coated her tongue and she swallowed it. The taste made her clit swell further, begging for attention. She slid a hand between her legs to stroke herself. Her fingers had made no more than one full circle when she felt his hand upon hers.

In the next moment, Connell shifted to the side, pushing at her hip in the same motion. He rolled her so skillfully she did not lose him from her mouth. He settled himself full on his back, hands on her hips and her heat poised over his mouth.

She paused in her sucking when she felt his breath upon her. Then the next minute her own cry burst from her throat at the sensation of his tongue licking her. Heat on heat, wet on wet, he circled her clit then kissed her. Soft, firm kisses. The tip of his tongue stroked her button.

She lost her concentration at first from the sheer ecstasy of it. It had been so long. So long even since she'd made love to herself. She couldn't breathe or move, could only let the glory of Connell's mouth upon her wash over her.

His hands stroked her hips, urging her to rock them in time to his kisses. This made it easier. She took him in her mouth again and let him move her body. Back and forth. He licked her while she sucked him.

She couldn't think. Could do nothing but ride the waves of pleasure. Her rhythm stuttered. She lost her place. Her hips moved against him until at last his hands held her still and he licked and licked and her entire body shook with climax. Her fingers clutched the bed clothes. She put her forehead to his thigh, her hair falling down over them, tangling round his cock, slick from her mouth.

His tongue fluttered on her. She broke. She shook. She came so hard she couldn't even think.

He rolled them again. She became aware of the softness of his bed beneath her back and the weight of his head upon her belly. He was stroking a hand along her hip and side, over and over. She blinked and looked down to see him looking up.

Grinning.

"Come here," she said, and he did at once.

She tasted her joy on his lips, and it made her shiver again. She held him close to her. He settled between her legs, his belly against her still-pulsing center. He pushed her hair off her face. He kissed her mouth, her cheeks, her eyes, her forehead, then rested his forehead against hers and looked into her eyes.

"I love you, Ella."

"I love you, too, Connell."

He smiled and kissed her once more, like he couldn't get enough of her, and she understood because she felt the same. She thought he would enter her, but he did not. Connell seemed content to lie upon her, kissing her, and Elspeth was content to let him.

She did not think her body could respond again to him. Her climax had left her shaken. But as Connell kissed her, soft, hard, gentle and fierce, once again heat pooled between her legs. Her body became pinpoints of sensation. Her lips. Her nipples, crushed against his chest. Her clit rubbed the firmness of his stomach.

Connell shifted, still kissing her, never stopping. The tip of his cock nudged her. She sighed and tilted her hips to aid his entrance. He did not push inside her.

Instead, he kissed her more. His hips made slow, gentle thrusts. His pelvic bone rubbed her clitoris with maddening continuity. His hand slipped round beneath her neck to hold her head as he kissed and kissed and kissed her.

Tongues stroked. Lips nibbled. Mouths opened, breath passing from one to the other. She no longer knew where she ended and he began. She no longer cared. She didn't know the moment he began to fill her, only that he slid the tip of his cock along her folds. She arched to take him further. He withdrew.

Their bodies had joined, melded by sweat and the slickness of her arousal. Nothing scraped, nothing pinched, nothing caught or tugged. Everything had become smoothness, like silk, like oil. Liquid and languid and flowing.

He slid inside her without pause. His cock nudged the entrance to her womb. His belly teased her clit. He began to move.

She heard herself murmuring his name, words of love, and heard him answer, but they came with no conscious effort on her part. They slipped from her lips as easily as breath. She could not think of words, could think of nothing but him moving inside her and his mouth on hers. Nothing else mattered.

"Ella—"

His surprised tone made her open her eyes. The air glimmered around them. The thrall filled her, making sight replace sound, sound become taste, taste transform itself to sight. Connell tasted like singing and smelled like sunshine. She had covered them both with the high magic without knowing it.

He moved faster with long, smooth strokes. The thrall glimmered and shimmered around them both. Her hands ran down his back to cup his rounded buttocks as he pushed upward on his hands to keep his weight from crushing her. Elspeth angled her hips and hooked her ankles around the back of his calves, urging him forward.

"Look at what you've done." Connell shivered. Sweat dripped from him. She slid her hands up his chest to tweak his nipples. "Look at you,

Ella. Look what you can do."

The thrall danced within her and around her. Connell did not have magic. She wanted to share it with him.

"Kiss me," she said.

He did. It should not have happened. It wasn't supposed to happen. Everyone said it could not happen.

Yet when he kissed her, it did. He opened to her out of love, and she gave him what she was feeling, seeing, tasting, smelling. He had no magic, but she gave him some of hers.

His eyes opened, glazed with passion, and she lost herself in his love. They moved together. He bent to kiss her again. He tasted like love. Together, they made love while the thrall covered them and urged them on, taking them higher.

I love you!

He answered her thought with his voice. "I love you, too. My Ella."

His pace became ragged. His breath shortened, and hers did, too. Starlight filled her, tension coiling, every part of her focused between her legs where the pressure built and built until it let go and she surged with climax again.

Connell thrust inside her once, twice, the last time falling forward to bury his face in her neck. He cried her name and gathered her into his arms.

His cock pulsed inside her. The thrall let her feel his seed filling her. Connell's climax sounded like moonlight and tasted like thunder, and it left her gasping and quaking with a third and final orgasm of her own.

The thrall had never filled her the way it just had. Connell rolled off to lie beside her, his head next to hers, his lips pressed against her shoulder. Elspeth lifted her hand and formed an orb. 'Twas perfect, without flaw, a deep and gleaming gold tinged with blue the color of summer sky.

She closed her fingers and it absorbed into her skin. She made another, as perfect as the first. This one she released. It hovered above them, waiting for her to command.

'Twas almost too much. She closed her fingers again and withdrew the orb. Her body hummed. Every sensation remained colored by a new awareness. By the thrall. By the magic Connell's love had let her access at last.

Elspeth began to weep.

"Ella, love, what's wrong?"

How could she explain how it felt to hold the thrall in her hands rather than have it slip away from her grasp? To know she could do anything now, make anything happen, create and destroy. How could she tell him, who had no magic, how the years of working so hard to harness what she'd been born to do had left her convinced she would never be able to do it?

How could she explain to one who did not have magic how empty she had been, and how full she was now?

"Ella?"

She looked down at him and brought him to her again for a kiss. "Thank you, Connell. Oh, thank you."

His brow furrowed at her tears, but he held her in his arms and kissed them away. "Shh, love. Please don't cry."

How could she explain that she wept from joy, not grief? That she had found her way at last along the path she'd thought never to walk. How could she tell him she had believed she would always be alone.

She could not. Numbers, not words, were her strength. She could not find the means to tell Connell everything in her heart.

She could only tell him what she'd already said. "I love you."

And 'twas enough, because he demanded no more from her. Her words were not inadequate to him. They were enough. At last, for her, everything was enough.

Everything counts in large amounts.

UNEXPECTED

UNEXPECTED

MOONLIGHT MADNESS

UNEXPECTED

UNEXPECTED

MOONLIGHT MADNESS

"One night only!" the sign screamed. The letters, so dark a red they looked almost black, glistened in the light of the full moon. "Moonlight Madness! Prices Slashed!"

Rhea paused. The alley was silent, except for the faint sound of water dripping from the fire escape onto cracked and dirty pavement. She had only meant to duck through here quickly on her way to the nightclub, but the promise of a bargain beckoned her.

She shrugged, looking around. The night was young. Nobody was waiting for her at the club anyway. Nobody was ever waiting for her.

She ducked into the shop, pushing back the hood of her faded black raincoat and lifting her hair free of the collar. It was humid inside the small store, and she felt her hair begin to instantly frizz. *Great.*

An odd smell hung in the air. Somehow familiar, yet she couldn't quite think of what it was. For some reason it made her think of summers at her grandfather's Golden Retriever kennel.

"May I help you?" A voice came from the shadows behind the low counter along the shop's narrow side wall.

Rhea jumped, not really startled and annoyed to find herself acting like she was. "I saw your sign," she said, rather lamely and instantly embarrassed. *Not that I have any reason to be,* she told herself sternly. The clerk didn't know her from a hole in the ground.

"Ah."

Now, for the first time, Rhea looked around the shop's crowded interior. Clothing racks packed it from end to end, all hung with coats of every kind of fur imaginable. That was the smell, she realized, wrinkling her nose while looking around in utter amazement. Not a bad smell. More like wet dog than anything else.

And no wonder, since it had been raining for nearly a week without pause. Everything had been damp for days, and the humidity was terrible. Other than the smell, the moisture in the air didn't seem to be affecting the garments in this store. She reached one hand out to stroke the soft fur of the coat nearest her. It looked like mink.

"A lovely choice," the voice behind the counter said, its owner still in shadow.

"You're having a sale?" She let the sleek fur drop. Stuff like this you found in Macy's or Bloomingdale's, not some dumpy shop in an alley. Well, this wouldn't be the first time she'd seen things that had "fallen" off the back of a truck. "What's the occasion?"

"Tonight's the full moon," the clerk said. "Have to move out the inventory."

Rhea strained her eyes to see the owner of the voice, but could only make out the vaguest of forms. "Your sign said prices slashed."

"Yes," the clerk replied. "For the right customer."

"And am I the right customer?" The coquettish tone of her voice irritated her. Where had that come from? Rhea had long ago learned no matter how many times she fluttered her eyelashes or shoved out her chest, she was no bombshell.

A low, dark chuckle that made the fine hairs on the back of her neck stand on end curled out of the dark. "Perhaps. Step into the light."

She took two steps forward before angrily catching herself. The clerk was still shielded in darkness, but now Rhea stood in what seemed to be a theater-strength spotlight. The brightness made her squint her eyes shut in protest, and made the clerk's dim form nearly impossible to make out.

"Look, buddy," Rhea said, and was perturbed to hear an edge of near-hysteria in her voice. "I don't know what you think you're trying to do…."

"Skinny," the clerk hissed. There came a sharp noise, like long nails tapping speculatively on the counter top. "Frizzy hair. Freckles. Some would call them the Devil's Spittle. Men don't flock around you much."

Rhea flinched, throwing up one hand to cover her eyes against the brightness. She knew she was no beauty queen, but this frank appraisal of her physical appearance was like a slap. Surprisingly, and infuriatingly, she felt hot tears spring into her eyes.

"Who...who the hell do you think you are?" she quavered.

"Hell, indeed," the clerk's low voice rumbled, and she swore he laughed.

Rhea had had enough. No fur coat, no matter how luxurious and no matter how cheap, was worth this sort of freak stuff. First the deserted shop, and next the creepy clerk making her feel ugly. She had a nightclub to get to, and even though she knew she would probably spend the night dancing alone, at least it was better than this.

"Wait," the clerk said, and she saw his dim form move from behind the counter. "I have just the coat for you."

"I don't want it," Rhea retorted, lifting her chin.

"Yes, you do."

He moved out from behind the counter, and despite herself, Rhea drew in her breath. He was magnificent, moving with a fluid grace unusual in such a powerfully built man. His dark hair was shoulder-length and shot through with gray. His eyes were a piercing, feral black. And his mouth, she marveled, was a slash of red the color of strawberries. He was the handsomest man she had ever seen, even though his over-thick eyebrows met above the sharpness of his nose, and the shadow on his cheeks was several hours past five o'clock.

He motioned to her with a smile that showed the whiteness of his teeth. "Come. Back here."

She followed him silently, weaving through the racks of fur that brushed her on every side. As they neared the back of the shop, Rhea cast a nervous glance over one shoulder. The guy, handsome though he might be, was weird. And they were alone. And nobody knew she was here.

"Ah," the clerk said, stopping finally at the back wall. "Here. Perfect."

Though the wall held enough hooks to hang a dozen coats, only one garment adorned the plaster. Rhea took a long, slow breath. She'd never imagined a coat like that.

The coat was fashioned from what appeared to be the entire pelt of the largest wolf she had ever seen. The fur was thick and shaggy, coarse yet with a luxurious sheen that made her want to run her fingers through it. Black, shot through with gray, just like the clerk's hair. The wolf's head formed the hood, so when the wearer pulled it up, the jaw would frame her face. Crimson satin lined the inside.

"It's gorgeous," Rhea said, moving forward to touch it.

"It's yours," the clerk said. Again, he flashed his teeth at her.

She shook her head, pulling away reluctantly. "I couldn't possibly afford anything like that. It must cost a fortune."

He named a price that made her laugh out loud.

"You're joking, right?" she asked bitterly. She knew about jokes, all right. She'd had them played on her many times, mostly by frat boys or businessmen who bet each other on who could find the homeliest girl and trick her into thinking she was something. Oh, yeah, she knew all about jokes.

"I never joke about my coats," the clerk said. He took the coat down from its hanger and held it out to her. "Try it on."

Though on the wall it had looked far too large, Rhea found the coat a perfect fit. The crimson satin caressed her bare arms. She twirled in front of the mirror, trying to see herself from every angle.

"It's like it was made for me," she whispered, enthralled by the sight of herself.

"Perhaps it was," the man said, and pulled the hood up around her face.

The fur framed her skin, blending with the fall of her hair and making it seem less frizzy, less flyaway. The snout peeped over her forehead like some kind of ornament, an exotic adornment that should have looked like something out of a tacky horror film...but somehow, didn't.

"You look like a queen." The clerk stroked the fur.

"No," she said, though she really meant yes.

"And how does it make you feel?"

Rhea's lips parted, but she couldn't speak, really. Watching her reflection, she saw herself. But not herself. A woman in a fabulous fur coat, with a handsome man behind her. She couldn't pull her gaze away from the sight.

"Lovely," the clerk whispered, his dark eyes catching hers in the mirror.

He ran his hands down her fur-covered sides, ruffling the coat. Then he slid his hands around the front of her, parting the heavy material to expose her dress beneath. *I ought to stop him,* she thought, idly, as his hand found the material of her skirt and began to inch it up past her thighs. All she could do was watch.

His other hand cupped her breast, thumbing the nipple until it stood upright, clearly visible through the thin cloth of her dress. She wore no bra. He pinched the taut button. She moaned.

"Does that make you wet?"

She nodded, speechless, knees weak. The clerk smiled, baring teeth that seemed too white. Too sharp. Like the teeth of the creature that had given its life for this coat.

The next moment, she felt just how sharp those teeth were on the side of her neck. The clerk pushed the hood out of the way with his face and nibbled the soft skin at the curve of her shoulder. Her nipples had been erect before, but now they could have cut glass. Stone. Steel.

She would have gasped, had she been able to breathe. As it was, her breath burned in her throat. The hand on her breast continued to tease and taunt her nipple, while his other hand inched her dress up to expose the lace triangle of her panties. She wore no hose, preferring bare legs for dancing.

His fingers traced lazy circles on her clit through the lace. If he hadn't been holding her, she'd have fallen for sure. Rhea watched, mesmerized, as he found just the right rhythm to get her going, without effort, without hesitation.

"You...." She spoke like she had a mouthful of syrup, every word liquid and oozing. A protest? It should have been, but wasn't. More like an assent.

"Hush," said the clerk, his finger circling, circling. "Watch and see what they will see tonight when they look at you wearing this coat."

And she did—she saw a woman everyone would turn their heads to watch pass by. Skin like cream, hair like flames, every freckle a beauty mark. Breasts like melons, taut cherry nipples, belly a sloping, curving, rounded plane that invited worship. Her sex, a treasure to be sought.

His teeth dimpled the flesh of her neck, but didn't break the skin. Surface tension, a water droplet hanging on the edge of the faucet, stretching, ready to drop...that was how she felt watching him almost, but not quite, draw blood; almost, but not quite, slip his finger inside her panties and finger her erect clit.

"Women will want to be you. Men will want to fuck you." He breathed the words into her skin, tasting her with every word, his tongue hot and wet against her. "Or perhaps the other way 'round, no? Now tell me how badly you want this coat."

"I want it."

His finger stroked, stroked her clit through the panties. Her hips moved as her head lolled back, her eyes glazing but not closing. She couldn't close them. She had to watch. Tension coiled in the pit of her belly. She licked her lips, watched, fascinated, as her tongue made her lips glisten.

"And what price would you pay for a coat this exquisite?"

He wasn't talking about money any longer. Rhea parted her thighs wider, leaning back against him. His finger moved, around and around, and every part of her became focused on that one small spot between her legs.

"If you want to get laid—"

"I don't." He grinned, feral and wild. Frightening.

His gaze locked on hers. His hand moved faster between her legs. Sensation whirled through her, pulling her tighter and tighter. Heat flooded her pussy as his strokes brought her to the edge.

"What do you want?" The words leaked out of her, a breathe/sigh/moan that might have embarrassed her under other circumstances.

"Nothing but this." He pinched her nipple, sending shudders through her. He tweaked her clit, making it throb. "To feel your pleasure."

"With nothing for you?"

He grinned, fingers stilling for a moment before starting to tap-tap against her button. The pressure/pause sensation stole her breath. Made her come, hard, within moments. She stumbled forward as he released her. The coat fell closed, covering her. Her orgasm washed through her, over her and around, and she closed her eyes against the sweetness of the pleasure.

"Now," said the clerk. "About the money."

Twenty minutes later, Rhea and the coat were on their way to the nightclub. Giddily, she hugged it around her, unbelieving. *The man must've been crazy,* she thought. Selling the coat to her for a price like that. Well, his loss and her gain. *It must have really been midnight madness after all.*

The bouncer took one look at her and the coat, and let her right in. Rhea, accustomed to waiting in line for hours, didn't question the man as he waved her through the doors. She wasn't about to tempt fate.

Inside, she was blasted with a wave of icy air that made her nipples peak against the thin cloth of her dress. Of course, after dancing for an hour or so, she'd be glad of the air conditioning that kept the humidity from kinking her hair and making her sweat. Right now, though, she was grateful for the wolf coat's heavy warmth.

There was a room, a closet really, where you could check your coat for a buck or two. Rhea glanced at it, but hesitated. Her old black raincoat had been worn and shabby enough to trust to the dubious safety of the coat room. This wolf coat was something different entirely. Though she had spent less to own it than she would to buy drinks tonight, the coat's value was priceless. She could not leave it in the care of the sallow-skinned, shifty-eyed clerk, who might be tempted let it go to someone else with more than a dollar to spend for its retrieval.

"Hey."

Rhea turned. The blond man towering over her was impeccably dressed and groomed, and smelled strongly of cologne. He smiled, his teeth glinting extra white in the blacklight accenting the nightclub's ceiling. He was handsome she had time to realize, before he had taken her hand.

"Dance with me."

"My...my coat," she began, already cursing her stumbling tongue. A hot flush crept over her chest and throat, and she blessed the dim lighting which obscured her embarrassment from his view.

"Leave it on," the Adonis before her said. "I like it."

Apparently every man at the club that night liked it, too. Rhea found herself passed from one gorgeous man to the next in dazed disbelief. They wanted her. Never had the snide looks of other women seemed so sweet, for now they stemmed from jealousy and not disdain. It was Rhea who was belle of the ball, Rhea who bumped and ground with one or several men at a time, and Rhea whose drinks were always fresh, always cold and always free.

Through it all she wore the coat, expecting to be overcome with heat. There was heat, all right, but it came from the men pressing their lean, muscled bodies against her, not the weight of the fur. The crimson satin was cool and smooth against her skin, the fur soft and coarse at the same time.

"You're driving me wild," the blond man, the one who had first drawn her onto the dance floor, said.

His name, she had learned, was Ted. He'd taken her to one of the barely lit booths lining the wall, where he'd dug his fingers into the coat's lush thickness, stroking it. Stroking her. He pulled the hood up so it framed her face. "God, you're like an animal!"

She didn't want to think about why being like an animal turned him on so much because that was just too weird. Instead, Rhea simply enjoyed the feeling of his mouth working against hers. Ted pulled her close to him, nibbling on her ear.

"I want you so bad," he whispered huskily and put her hand on his crotch.

Rhea stroked him through the material, thinking of how many times she'd been groped in dark corners by men like this. How often she'd traded strokes for drinks, for the few minutes of being made to feel wanted. How many dark corners like this one she'd come out of with smeared lipstick and tangled hair.

"Go down on me," she said suddenly.

To give him credit, Ted barely paused. "What? Here? Now?" he said around nibbling her jaw and throat.

"Here. Now."

She didn't think he would. She'd underestimated the power of the coat. Without another word, Ted slid off the seat to kneel in front of her. He pushed up her dress past her thighs and unerringly found her clit with his tongue, even through the lace of her panties. He stabbed at her flesh, prodding it with his tongue. He looked up at her briefly, eyes glazed, and swiped his tongue across his lips. He dove down again, pausing this time to tug down her panties. His lips found her. He kissed her pussy. Just kissed it, the same as he would her mouth, kissed it over and over until her clit swelled.

Then he began to tongue her in earnest. The fur on her hood tickled her face as she leaned her head back. The music pounded in her ears, echoing the thumping of her heart, which in turn echoed between her legs.

Damn, she thought, dazed from booze and exertion, the music making it hard to think. Ted knew what he was doing down there. He licked her in steady, smooth strokes, each one precise, centered on her clitoris. Every so often, just enough to keep her on edge, he did some sort of flutter-flip that had her pumping her hips against his mouth.

She'd never had oral sex like this. Any sex like this for that matter. Past lovers, if they'd deigned to go down on her, had done it with lackluster effort and little enthusiasm. Ted was making love to her pussy like it was the last thing he was ever going to do for the rest of his life.

Rhea groaned, the noise lost beneath the club's pounding soundtrack. *This coat,* she thought incoherently. *This coat fucking rocks!*

Ted slid a finger inside her, then another, twisting them while he fluttered his tongue against her clit. Rhea spread her legs farther, inviting him without words to keep working his magic. And, boy, did he ever.

Her orgasm inched closer and closer. Ted slid his hands under her ass, pushing his face against her, fucking her with his tongue and fingers and teeth…oh, mercy…teeth? She yelped, arching against him, the noise lost in the noise from the club.

She felt him chuckle against her, the vibrations rumbling through her pussy and sending her crashing over the edge into climax. Neon colored stars flashed in front of her closed eyes. The pounding of her heart drowned out the bass from the dance music.

"That is some coat," growled Ted into her ear.

Rhea sat up and flipped the coat closed over her front, then pulled him to her for a kiss. The taste of her on his lips sent another surge of arousal through her. "Take me home."

Rhea was no virgin. She had had her share of lovers, most of them picked up at this nightclub or others just like it. Sometimes the men she went home with were good looking, even attractive, though there had not been a Keanu Reeves among the lot of them. And they were always drunk.

Ted, on the other hand, was gorgeous. Rhea had always known her looks would never win any awards. What had the fur store clerk said? "Frizzy hair. Freckles. Men don't flock around you much." That had always been true…before tonight.

"Your place," Rhea said, and was surprised to hear the sultry, smoky tone of her own voice.

Now, with the wolf coat swirling around her ankles and Ted's lips against her throat, Rhea felt a thousand miles away from the woman who had ventured down that dripping alley just a few hours ago. She arched her chest against Ted's questing fingers and rubbed the bulge in his pants. He had said she was like an animal, and didn't she feel like one? Fierce and passionate? And…pretty?

They didn't even make it out the club door before he'd pushed her up against a wall and slid his hand beneath her skirt. His fingers inched down and found her slickness, left over from before, and Rhea let out a low moan. A growl, really, that surprised her and made Ted shudder against her while he tongued her neck. His finger stroked her once, twice, and her hips bucked on the verge of orgasm. He slipped one finger inside her, and she came like a freight train.

"C'mon," he whispered in her ear while she sagged against him in stunned satisfaction. "Let's get out of here."

Ted drove a Jaguar, a black one, and he drove it fast. Rhea opened all the windows, and let the night hair whip her hair and the fur of the wolf coat together until it was impossible to tell where she ended and the coat began. A howl rose in her throat and she let it out, amused at how the noise made Ted squirm in his seat. She pressed her fingers to his crotch and felt the throb of his arousal, and Rhea laughed, free like the animal he had called her. Free like a wolf.

Ted proved to be as skilled at lovemaking as he was at dancing and driving. Rhea wasn't surprised. It all had something to do with the coat.

They were scarcely in the door before he'd pushed her up against the wall, kissing her and running his hands up and down her sides. "Bedroom..." he mumbled. "That way."

Rhea turned her head to see a door at the end of the hall. The husky tone of her voice made her smile. "Can we make it that far, do you think?"

Ted huffed against her neck, lifting her skirt higher around her hips. "If we don't, we'll just have to fuck another time."

That did surprise her, enough to push him back. "Another time?"

Ted pulled away to look into her eyes. "Well, sure."

He seemed puzzled, running his mouth up and down her chin before pulling away again. "Don't you like me?"

"I don't even know you," Rhea replied.

"You could get to know me."

She laughed, throwing back her head and letting the coat ripple around her. Then she walked toward the bedroom, curling her finger for him to follow. "We'll see."

She'd never been in a position of such power before. A man actually insinuating he wanted more than just one night? She was sure, now that she had it, that she wanted that. This was too much fun.

"On the bed," she told him, looking around. Nice furniture, expensive. Black comforter on a white-painted bed. Well-chosen prints in black and white on the walls, which were white. Through another door she saw a bathroom, decorated in the same colors. He had quite a theme going on.

Obligingly, Ted went to the bed and stripped back the comforter to reveal plain sheets. Rhea grinned, walking toward him with a sway in her hips she'd never mastered before tonight. "Nice."

He grinned, stretching out on them, hands behind his head. "Thanks."

"Take off your clothes."

Still grinning, he sat up to undo the buttons on his shirt. He shrugged out of the shirt, revealing a chest rippling with muscles. The line of hair on his belly trailed over what she thought was called an eight-pack. *Yummy.*

"Never been with a man like you," she murmured, coming closer.

"Never been with a woman like you."

Rhea laughed and tossed her hair. "I believe that."

"No. I mean it. You're amazing."

That stopped her for a moment. She looked down at herself, at the coat, the soft fur beneath her fingers. He was being earnest. The kind of man who'd never have given her a passing glance before was now calling her amazing. What a fucking awesome coat! But her smile faded after a moment. She had to take it off sometime.

"Take off your pants," she said. "I want to see all of you."

Ted obliged, stripping off his trousers and tossing them to the floor, then pushing his boxers over his thighs and down. He stood up, hands on his hips, every inch of him perfection. His cock rose from a nest of hair the color of wheat, a bit darker than that on his head.

"Beautiful," she murmured.

Ted stroked it lightly, palming the head before moving back down the length. "I've been hard since I met you."

Rhea raised an eyebrow. "Must be awfully uncomfortable. Maybe I can help you with that."

She went to him and pushed him back onto the bed, then straddled him. The coat fell over both of them. He moaned. She moaned. Then she laughed.

Rhea bent to capture his mouth with hers, nibbling at his lips until he parted them. Her tongue darted inside, stroking, and his returned the favor. He put his hands around her, under the heavy fur. He ran them up and down the fabric of her dress.

Rhea slid down his body, kissing and nibbling and sucking, until she reached the beauty of his erection and slid it down her throat. Her lips touched the base of it, his curling pubic hair tickling her nose. He throbbed inside her mouth. She smiled as she slid her mouth up and over the head of his prick, adding a bit of extra suction at the tip.

Ted muttered an expletive that made her chuckle. His hand found her hair, tangled in it, and pulled gently. "I'm going to come if you keep doing that."

She sat up to look at him. "That's the point, isn't it?"

Ted blinked lust-glazed eyes. "But I want to make love to you first."

For a moment, she only stared at him. "All right."

He'd already given her multiple explosive orgasms, but Ted seemed intent on providing her with even more. Without regard to his own pleasure, which was a concept that frankly boggled Rhea's brain. No man, ever, had taken the time to do the things he was doing to her without expecting something in return.

"I want to make love to you on top of it," Ted told her, stripping off the heavy fur and tossing it down on his bed.

The fur on their bodies seemed to spur them both on in ways Rhea had never even imagined. Ted went down on her again, licking her to yet another mind-blowing orgasm, and while she was still shuddering beneath him he slid inside her. He kissed her thoroughly, tasting her lips, before he began to move. When he did, when he began to thrust, each movement was exquisite, like a carefully orchestrated dance designed to send her to the heights of ecstasy.

"I want to feel you come around me," he whispered in her ear.

Never in a million years would Rhea have thought her body capable of such a thing. Yet when he moaned her name as he moved inside her, she responded. Again, the shivers of climax rippled through her, and she dug her nails into his back, grabbing his ass to shove him harder into her.

He rolled so she ended up on top of him. The cool air caressed her. She hooked her fingers in the hem of her dress and pulled it up over her head, throwing it to the floor. Now she was naked, too. Her unbound breasts bounced with every thrust. Rhea let her head loll back; let the rising sensation flood through her.

"I can't come again. It's impossible!" She cried the words even as she felt familiar stirrings inside her.

"Anything is possible!"

She laughed, gloriously, riding him as another wave of pleasure made her head spin. On and on through the night they rutted like beasts, up and down and in positions she bet the Kama Sutra hadn't heard of. She had orgasm after mind-blowing orgasm, and Ted's cries of ecstasy let her know he was feeling the same.

How lucky to be a woman, Rhea thought drowsily when, at last, Ted had thrust his final thrust and screamed his final scream, collapsing on top of her in a cloud of Drakkar and sweat. Surely multi-orgasms were God's way of making up for the hassle of periods and childbirth and all the other indignities which women faced. Yes, she was lucky to be a woman, especially after a night like that.

She woke to see the light of morning streaming through the windows. Somewhere a shower was droning on and on. She heard singing. *That would be Ted,* Rhea thought with a lazy stretch. He didn't sing as well as he screwed.

She rolled to her side, meaning to fling out her hand and caress the coat which had changed her whole life. Instead of the plush, rich fur, however, Rhea's fingers slid across skin. If Ted was in the shower, who was in the bed?

She blinked twice, slowly. It was not Ted in the bed with her. It was still the coat, but it had changed.

"Shit," Rhea said. It was just her sort of luck. "No wonder it was on sale."

The hood was still there, and the arms, and even the crimson lining. Now, however, the red cloth was sewn to a different sort of skin. A man's skin. His hair was black shot through with gray.

Whoever had processed the skin had done an excellent job, for he was still in one piece from head to foot. The arms had been hollowed and stretched cleverly to form the arms of the coat. The only imperfection in the skin was where the jaw split to form a hood, which when pulled over the wearer's head would frame the face.

All in all, it was a magnificent piece of craftsmanship, and an incredibly unique garment…even if she'd only get to wear it once a month, when the moon was full.

UNEXPECTED

MONSTER IN THE CLOSET

UNEXPECTED

UNEXPECTED

MONSTER IN THE CLOSET

Tessa Hanson had a naked man in her closet. She peered downward. A very well-endowed naked man. She blinked, and then blinked again. He didn't disappear.

"Boo," he said.

She closed the door and stared at it for a moment. She heard the rattle of hangers and some muffled thumps. When she opened it again, he was still there.

"Boo," the naked man repeated.

Dreaming. She had to be dreaming. With a shake of her head, Tessa tried to close the closet door again. This time, the naked man put a large hand between the door and the jamb.

"Wait," he said. "I *know* I can scare you."

"Who the hell are you?"

"It doesn't matter who I am," he said. "Look, just go back to bed and let me try again, okay? Only this time, wait until I've opened the door the whole way before you wake up."

This was really too much. Tessa gave a narrow-eyed squint toward the faintly glowing clock on her bedside table. It was way, way too early in the morning for her to be awake. She put her hands on her hips and faced the intruder.

Hung like a horse or not, this guy was working her very last nerve. "What?"

With a backward glance, the man catapulted himself out of the closet and kicked the door shut behind him. The force of his flight knocked Tessa over, and they both fell onto the bed. Tessa found herself with a face full of fragrant male chest, complete with curling dark hair and rippling muscles.

She gave his skin an experimental lick. Yum. He tasted good, too. She reached around and gave his firm, muscled ass a squeeze.

"Hey!" The man rolled off her and jumped up. "Stop that!"

Tessa sat up and scrubbed at her face. She looked at the clock again. Two more minutes had passed, bringing her two minutes closer to the time her alarm would ring.

"If this is one of those sex dreams," she said pleasantly, "do you think we could get started? I have an early appointment tomorrow morning."

"Dream?" It appeared she'd stunned him. His eyes flashed, reflecting the green glow from her clock. "No! This—you don't understand."

Annoyed again, Tessa crossed her arms over her chest. "Then what the hell, exactly, is going on? I wake up because I hear something in my closet, and I find you. Naked. It's clear to me this can't be really happening, so of course I assume it's a sex dream, especially since you just threw me down on the bed."

"No, no, no." The man shook his head. "This isn't a dream."

His dark hair fell in silky-looking lengths to his broad shoulders. *The kind of hair a woman would like to feel drifting across her thighs,* Tessa thought. The last few men Tessa had dated wore business suits, kept their nails trimmed, used hair products, worked out.

Metrosexuals, she thought the new term was, for men who required as much, if not more, personal care than the women they dated. This sleek, muscled hunk with the Samurai hair and burning gaze was just what she'd been missing.

"If it's not a dream," she said slowly, "then what were you doing in my closet?" *What a drool-worthy body.*

The intruder began to pace along the side of her bed. Nice pecs, to-die-for abs, an ass she'd already discovered was perfectly made for squeezing. Long, muscled legs, and yep, she peeked down toward the floor. Nice toes.

He'd said something, but she was so caught up in her appraisal of his body, Tessa hadn't heard it. "What?"

"I'm supposed to scare you," he said rather miserably.

"Scare me?" She looked him over again, taking the time to really check out his package. Damn. His kickstand could've held up a Harley.

"Naked?"

He looked down, as if just noticing. "Oh. Crap."

"You didn't know you were naked?"

He looked up and his eyes met hers. They were green, she realized. Not emerald, or jade, not even grass green. Glowing green. Like the numbers on her clock.

"I forgot to put on the uniform."

"Uniform?" Tessa shook her head to clear away the cobwebs. She got to her feet to confront him. "What are you talking about?"

He sighed heavily. "I'm the monster in your closet."

Surely she hadn't heard correctly. "You're the what in my what-what?"

He looked at her like he was defying her to contradict him. "I am the monster in your closet. I'm supposed to scare you. Only I forgot the uniform because I was running late. I figured you wouldn't know the difference—that I could just scare you and leave, collect my pay and be done with it. But you didn't get scared," he said accusingly. "And now I'm screwed. I'm going to have to go back to sprinkling fairy dust and painting rainbows, and let me tell you, lady, there's no fucking future in rainbows."

Taken aback, Tessa said the only thing she could think of. "Would it help if I screamed?"

The look he gave her made shivers run up and down her spine like fingers plucking a harp's strings. "It might."

Tessa clamped her thighs shut tight on her perking-up pussy. Slickness teased her with every movement, and she became suddenly very aware of her clitoris, which previously had been contentedly nestled, asleep, and now apparently had decided to sit up and take a look around. She opened her mouth and let out a yelp. "Help! Eek! Oh, how frightening!" She lowered her voice to a confidential whisper. "How was that?"

"You didn't sound very scared," the man muttered. "Oh, just forget it."

He sat on Tessa's bed and put his head in his hands. Uncertain of what to do, Tessa sat beside him and put her hand on his shoulder. His skin was warm and smooth, like heated satin.

"You don't feel like a monster," she murmured.

He looked up at her. "Closets normally aren't my gig. I told you—"

"Fairy dust and rainbows. I know." Tessa slid her fingers from his shoulder down his bare arm to rest them on his wrist. "That doesn't sound so bad."

"No?" The man got to his feet and stood in front of her, gesturing at his gorgeous body. "Do I look like I should be flitting around from flower to flower, sprinkling glitter on rosebuds?"

She let herself admire his luscious build for a moment before she answered. "No, but you don't look like you should be lurking in closets either."

"It's supposed to be a part-time job," he explained, like that somehow would make better sense. "Just a foot in the right department. You wouldn't believe how hard it is to get hired without experience."

She thought of her own corporate struggle. "Not much call for closet monsters any more?"

He sat down beside her again, his body warmth like a fire against her side. His eyes glowed brighter with excitement. "There's plenty of work for closet monsters. I'm in training to be an incubus."

Tessa burst out laughing. "You're kidding me."

The man shook his head. "No, really. The hours are great, the pay is excellent, and the benefits are amazing."

Tessa peeked down at his long, thick cock nestled between strong thighs. "I bet."

His gaze followed hers. "But you have to complete a very intensive training program first. So far, I've managed to get to the closet monster level."

Tessa cleared her throat. "Ummm…"

"Magnus."

"Magnus. And what, exactly, do you need to do to finish the training?"

He grinned. She'd thought him handsome before, in a somewhat disturbing way, but he became devastating now. "I have to perform a seduction that changes someone's life."

"That's it?"

He frowned. "It's not as easy as it sounds. You'd be surprised how easy it is to get into a woman's bed these days."

Tessa looked again the chest, the abs, the thighs… "I wouldn't be so surprised."

"It's the life change part that really matters, and that's the hard part." Magnus sighed again. "The corporate office is very strict about what constitutes a life change. I took the monster job as a way to get myself in front of the right people, maybe get offered an internship. But I blew it."

Tessa put her hand on his shoulder again. "What if I blew it instead?"

His head swiveled to stare at her. "What?"

Tessa licked her lips and looked pointedly down between his legs. "I haven't had sex in two years, Magnus. The closest I've been to a real penis was a perv who flashed me in the park last month. I'm horny as hell and looking at you is like holding up a plate of pasta in front of someone on a low-carb diet."

He drew back, just a little. "I'm not licensed yet to perform seductions."

Tessa moved her hand on his thigh, her fingertips only inches away from that luscious, delicious, tantalizing cock. "It looks like you've got all the right equipment to me."

He laughed, low and breathy, like her suggestion had turned him on and embarrassed him. "You can't be serious."

"I'm completely serious, Magnus." Tessa slid her hand up to his belly, then higher, to rub his taut nipples.

He captured her hand with his and held it tightly. His glowing gaze bore into hers. His tongue swiped across his lips.

"I have to be the one doing the seducing," he said. "Or it doesn't count."

She relaxed her fingers in his grip. "Okay." She waited, but he didn't move. "Magnus?"

He cleared his throat, still staring deeply into her eyes. "You do know what you're getting yourself into, don't you? You know what an incubus is?"

"A demonic sexual predator who steals into women's dreams and fucks them senseless?" Her own tone had gone husky and hopeful.

Magnus dipped his head a little closer until, with each word he spoke, his lips brushed hers. "Common misconception. Incubi aren't always demons. Most of the time, they're fae folk like me."

Tessa's head fell back and her lips parted, waiting for his tongue to slide between them. "Fae?"

He put her hand to the side of his face. She circled her fingers on the soft lobe of his ear, then up a little higher to caress the pointed tip. Magnus flicked her lips with his tongue and when she gasped, slipped inside her mouth to tantalize without really kissing her.

"What are you? Elf?"

"Fae," he corrected and slid his tongue along her jaw, then nipped the tender spot below her ear. "But it's politically incorrect to differentiate between the species."

Tessa's nipples had perked into tight, hard buds at his touch. When he put his hands on her breasts, she cried out softly. Hot moisture pooled between her thighs. It had been a long, long time.

"What about the rest of it?" she managed to squeak. "The fucking senseless part?"

"Oh, that." His gentle sucking on her neck sent pulses of pleasure directly to her swollen clit. "That part's absolutely correct."

She groaned. His hand moved between her thighs, bare beneath the oversized T-shirt she'd worn to bed. He stroked her through her cotton panties, found the erect button of her clitoris, and pressed it gently as he continued to nibble and suck her neck and throat.

Her hips lifted and her arm curled around his neck. The soft material of her nightshirt pulled and dragged on her over-sensitized nipples, creating a delightful push-pull of friction that drove her mindless with desire, but refused to sate it.

"You're supposed to resist me at first," Magnus reminded.

"No," Tessa said. "Stop. Don't. Oh. Oh. Oh!"

His chuckle sent bursts of heat flaming through her. He slid one finger beneath the elastic leg band of her panties and found her slick folds at the same time he left her neck and found her mouth.

He kissed her this time—really kissed her—and his tongue slid between her lips as his finger slid into her pussy.

Magnus swallowed her cry of passion. His finger moved inside her, joined quickly by another, and Tessa lifted herself upward to allow him as much access to her body as he could get. With the barrier of her nightshirt and panties still between them, her skin ached for his touch.

Magnus murmured some words she didn't understand, and all at once, she was as bare as he.

"Nice trick," Tessa gasped, still impaled on his fingers. He'd added his thumb to press on her button while he finger-fucked her, and she was surprised to find she could form coherent words.

"I've got dozens," Magnus whispered. "Want to see another one?"

He didn't wait for her answer, just did something with his hand that made her yelp with pleasure. His cock, hard as marble, pressed against her belly. He rubbed her with it and the head nudged the underside of her breasts. Her nipples scraped his chest.

The slickness coating her thighs allowed him to slide a third finger into her pussy. His thumb tap-tapped on her clit. Bright sparks of light flashed in her vision.

"I'm going to come!"

Magnus shook his head. "No, you aren't."

She moaned and wriggled. "Oh, yes, yes, yes! I am!"

He withdrew his fingers. "No, you're not. Not until I let you."

"Not fair."

He leaned in, licked her lips, and teased her with his tongue. "It wouldn't be much of a seduction if you climaxed within the first five minutes."

That cooled her jets a little bit. "Are you saying I'm too easy?"

He slid a hand along her hip, then up to cup her breast. Her nipple pebbled against his palm, and she moaned, she groaned, her body shuddered.

"Yes."

"It's been a really long time," Tessa found the voice to say.

Magnus nodded solemnly. "All the more reason for this to take a bit longer, isn't it?"

The only longer she wanted to take was his rod all the way inside her. She reached down to grip it, only to find herself flat on her back, hands pinned above her head. His glowing green eyes burned into hers, and she licked her lips nervously. The man was fae, after all, and even though Tessa wasn't quite sure what that meant, she thought it sounded like it could be dangerous.

"Are you afraid of me?"

Tessa lied. "No."

He chuckled again. The sound rumbled through her tummy and centered in her still throbbing clitoris, which spasmed. She clenched her legs.

"It's perfectly normal to be afraid." Magnus dipped his head to lick and nibble her throat. "I can feel your heart beating."

Tessa felt it, too, hammering in her chest like a runaway freight train. She tried to shift, but Magnus' strong hands held her tightly in place. His body pinned hers. His cock rubbed against her belly when he moved to kiss her lips.

She opened her mouth to speak, maybe to protest again, and his tongue swept inside, silencing her. She arched beneath him, opening her legs, wanting him to slide inside her, impale her, fuck her senseless as he'd promised. Her pussy contracted again and again in pre-come spasms prompted by the delicious feel of his bare cock on her naked flesh. She writhed and moaned under him, and tilted her hips upward, but still, Magnus didn't slide inside her.

"Damn you," she muttered.

"Can't," he replied matter-of-factly. "I'm fae, not demon, remember?"

All at once, she'd had enough. If he wasn't going to fuck her, he was just wasting her time. Demon or faery, whatever the hell he was, he was no better than a tease. Tessa tensed her body, gathered her will and bucked him upward in a move she'd learned in self-defense class. As Magnus flew forward, she hooked her leg around his, grabbed his shoulder, and flipped him over. She ended up with her knee wedged against the base of his still-bare, now very tender balls and her hands pressing down on his biceps.

"Listen," she growled, putting her face close to his. "I'm tired and horny. Quit fooling around and do what you came here to do, or get the hell out!"

Magnus stared, his glowing eyes narrowed. "I could throw you off. If I wanted to."

"Yeah?" Tessa let go of his arms and slid upward, so her slick pussy rubbed along his thick, hard cock. "Why don't you?"

Before he could answer, she'd slid herself down onto him, engulfing him. The moan ripped from her throat, a sound of long-awaited satisfaction. Her entire body shuddered. Her clit came to rest against the muscled ridges of his belly, and she moved just enough to tease the small bead of flesh into further arousal.

"You..." His voice was hoarse. He blinked. "That's not..."

"Shut up," Tessa whispered, leaning forward to lick him from chin to forehead. "And fuck me."

At her command, Magnus' hands found her hips and he began to move. He pumped in and out of her, fiercely, just the way she wanted it. Tessa cried out, sat up, and took him all the way inside her. Her breasts bobbed as he slammed into her, over and over. One of his hands came around to thumb her clit, and she burst into flames, into shards of glass, into rose petals scattered on the wind. She separated and returned to herself in the span of a heartbeat, then another, and her body bucked and jerked from the force of her orgasm.

After a minute, when she could think again, Tessa realized Magnus hadn't finished. He moved slower now, at a gentler pace that didn't rock her entire body. A small tilt of the hips, supplemented with a gentle roll of his pelvis, kept him sliding in and out without overwhelming her.

His gaze pinned hers. His thumb pressed on her button.

Oh, my. She was going to come again.

As soon as the thought crossed her mind, Magnus shifted the steady pressure, made it lighter, less direct. Less frequent. Teasing her again. Tessa bore down on him, clenching him with her inner muscles, trying to force him to give her what her body was now craving once more.

He wouldn't do it. His grin infuriated her and she reached down to stroke herself, but Magnus grabbed her hand. "Seduction," he reminded her.

"Fuck your seduction," Tessa growled. "I want this. I need this!"

He held her wrist so tightly she couldn't pull away. "And I want to be an incubus. If you do this the right way, we can both benefit."

She stared him down, her chest heaving with the panting breaths she slowed only by force of will. He didn't even blink. That glowing green glare didn't waver. Tessa sighed, finally, her body still in an upheaval of lust and hormones.

She thought of the many times her boss, Norman Finkbein, had accused her of not being a team-player. Her last lover, Hank Fresca, had told her she was an "I" not a "we" person just before he left her. Now Magnus was offering her more amazing sex…if only she bent a little. Gave in a little bit.

"All right," she agreed. "What do you need me to do?"

"Haven't you ever let anyone seduce you before?"

Tessa almost scoffed, but then she thought about it. She'd always been the aggressor in every relationship she'd ever had, business or pleasure. Her string of lovers had included men in nearly every profession, from cowboy to stock broker, but they'd all had one thing in common. Once she'd set her sights on them, it had only been a matter of time until she had them in her bed. In the office, she made and broke more deals in one day than most of her colleagues did in a week, and if something fell through, she passed it off with a shrug and moved on to the next. The same way she dealt with her lovers.

"You haven't. I can tell." Magnus slid a hand along her belly, up to tweak her nipple. "This tells me."

Tessa sighed, but restrained herself from leaning into his touch. He nodded approvingly and tweaked her upright nipple. She shuddered. Her clit ached for him to touch and stroke it, but she kept from thrusting her hips. His cock swelled inside her and she moaned a little.

"You take what you want, don't you?" His voice caressed her. "Have you ever waited for someone to give it to you first?"

"I'm not good with waiting." Her voice was breathy and low as she sat still, impaled on his rod.

Magnus put both hands on her hips and rolled her over way more gently than she'd done to him. When she settled onto her back on the bed, he withdrew and she bit her lip to hold back the low cry of frustration. Magnus parted her legs. His hot breath slid along her thighs, drifted over her pussy, swirled around her clitoris. His hands kept her hips still. He licked her.

Tessa squealed.

The tip of Magnus' tongue stroked her swollen clitoris in one, two, three smooth strokes. One finger, then another, slid inside her slick tunnel. He put his other hand beneath her ass to lift her upward, toward his mouth. His lips, his tongue, even his teeth danced on her love-starved flesh, but did not send her into orgasm.

"Fuck me," Tessa gasped.

"Seduction," returned Magnus' whisper, hot on her pussy. His fingers moved inside her. "Seduction, Tessa."

She hadn't told him her name. It didn't matter. All that mattered was his tongue on her clit and his fingers pumping in and out of her.

"Fuck me!"

What did he want from her? She'd allowed him to call the shots, hadn't she? Wasn't that seduction enough? What more did he possibly...oh...

Tessa arched her back as the beginnings of her orgasm flowed over her. Her thighs trembled and jerked. Her hips pumped, sending her upward against Magnus' mouth.

"Please, Magnus," she heard herself saying. "Make love to me."

She'd said the magic words. He left her pussy, but before she had time to protest, he'd seated himself inside her all the way to the base of his balls. She cried out again as his cock filled her so unexpectedly, but his kiss smothered her voice.

Magnus rolled his pelvis. His cock thrust. His belly muscles scraped and rubbed at her clitoris, and Tessa tilted her hips to match his pace, his pattern...oh, to match him. She took him in all the way and gave him all she had. Her body tensed.

She was coming.

Then, damn him, she wasn't.

She hovered on the brink for what seemed like an eternity. Everything around her faded away until all she saw was Magnus' eyes. The glowing green eyes.

They swept her away. She stood on a cliff, Magnus beside her, holding her hand. They both were naked. Below them, black waves crashed and roared on rocks as jagged and spiked as dinosaur teeth.

The water's movement echoed the ebb and surge of desire within her. Tessa shuddered and tried to pull her fingers away from Magnus, but his grip bore down on hers and she couldn't break free.

"Let me go!"

He shook his head, silently. He pointed at the waves. One rose up so high the spray splashed their bare toes. Tessa jumped back, held from running away by her fae lover.

"I don't want this!" The scream tore from her throat, burning. "Damn it, Magnus, I thought we were just supposed to fuck!"

"Life change," she thought she heard him whisper. The cliff disappeared. They stood in a forest, green and damp, fronds of fern hanging from prehistorically towering trees. The low grunt of an animal from the underbrush startled her into leaping forward. Magnus caught her. His skin was warm, hotter than the humid air around them.

"What's going on?"

"This is the fae realm." He nodded toward one huge tree, strung with cobwebs sparkling with dew. "This, and the other place, and thousands more."

Nudity had never bothered her before. Tessa worked hard to keep her body in good shape, and every line and scar, every wrinkle and freckle, was part of her. Her body wasn't perfect, but it was hers, and she had little patience for anyone who expected perfection.

Now, though, with Magnus' eyes assessing her, she crossed her arms over her breasts. He smiled. Heat shot through her and sent her still-tingling clit into a tiny spasm. She was still horny as hell, still on the cusp of climax. She'd never been aroused for so long without release.

"Why'd you bring me here?" she asked and forced her arms to her sides.

"I wanted to show you where I live." Magnus gestured.

They were no longer in a forest. Now a meadow stretched out all around them, with waving grass and masses of flowers for miles in all directions. Red, blue, purple, yellow, orange…the blossoms waved and danced in a scented breeze that lifted her hair from her neck and teased her nipples into erect points. The wind crept between her legs, licked at her clit and pussy, stroked her inner thighs until Tessa trembled and went to her knees.

"Why are you torturing me like this?" The question trickled out of her attached to a low moan.

She was eye-level to his erection. His cock looked absolutely good enough to eat, and even though he'd been a real bastard to her so far, Tessa wanted to take him inside her mouth, all the way down her throat, all the way until she could kiss his balls while she sucked him. In fact, she didn't think she'd ever wanted anything more in her entire life.

"You want me to wait for you to give," she told him. "But you don't give!"

"Demanding to be given is the same as taking it without waiting."

Tessa growled low in her throat. The sensual haze had overtaken her entire body, so that each limb felt infused with erotic hunger. Her hands ached to caress warm and willing flesh, her tongue longed to stroke and lick, her lips curved with the desire to suck and kiss.

The soft earth cradled her knees, while the flowers crushed under them gave off a strong, heady scent that made her head swim. She reached for him, expecting him to move out of her grasp and startled when she caught him.

Magnus seemed startled, too, but before he could step back, Tessa had moved forward and given in to her longing. His thick, ridged cock slid down the back of her throat and she loosened the muscles there to keep from choking. The taste of him filled her senses. The curly dark hair at the base of his penis tickled her lips and nose as she took him all the way. She let him slide back out and gave a bit of extra suction at the tip.

Magnus groaned. His strong thighs twitched against her shoulders. Her breasts rubbed against his shins. The grass and flowers sprang up between her legs and tickled and caressed her all over. Tessa tilted her hips to allow the petals rub against her own rosebud, back and forth.

She put her hands up to cup his ass. The muscles clenched and relaxed under her palms as he thrust in and out of her mouth. She was winning.

I'm going to make you come.

The thought filled her head, but Magnus answered her with his own.

No. This seduction is mine.

Tessa added a tongue flick and a nibble to her sucking and was triumphant when she forced another groan from his throat. His cock pulsed in her mouth. His balls tightened when she cupped them. She ran a finger down the soft sack and his hips jerked in response.

Is this a contest? she thought and gave another long suckle that had him groaning. *To see who comes first?*

You're not supposed—

Fuck your I'm not supposed to, she thought. *Your world or mine, it doesn't matter. The easiest way to get me to do something is to tell me not to!*

She'd been called selfish before, and Tessa could admit to thinking of herself first in many areas of her life, but sex was not one of them. She gave as much as she took, and not one of her lovers had ever walked away from her unsatisfied.

The meadow disappeared and they were on a beach while a calm blue sea lapped around her knees. Then a mountaintop, where snow made her shiver; then to a desert with sand as warm as Magnus' cock in her mouth.

He was close, she could tell, and her own climax could no longer be ignored. Tessa slipped a hand between her thighs and rocked against her palm. One stroke, then another, and she'd come.

But not before Magnus does.

The mountain disappeared. A jungle surrounded them, while a waterfall crashed into a clear, deep pool only a hand's breadth away. The ground was slick with water. Though she hadn't moved from her knees, she slipped anyway, just a little, but it was enough for Magnus to pull away.

As quick as that he grabbed her, flipped her, and plunged inside her. Tessa screamed, not in anger or even in fear. Pure ecstasy burst through her at the feeling of Magnus' cock filling her. She wrapped her legs around his waist and urged him closer.

He kissed her, mouth open, tongue plundering her with no tenderness. It drove her wild. Her fingernails raked down the smooth, hot skin of his back, and his eyes flared into a green inferno. His mouth found her throat and she tensed, arching her back, waiting for the sting of teeth. He nipped, then laved the spot with his tongue and sent ecstatic shudders racing through her.

She had never been so close to coming for so long, and now her body faltered. Stuck. She crested, reached for it, strained toward release, but still it didn't happen.

Magnus lifted his head to stare into her eyes again. This close she could see beneath the glow to the thick, dark lashes, the pale jade iris, and the ebony pupils dilated with passion.

"This doesn't have to be a contest," he breathed against her mouth. "You give…I'll take. You take…I'll give. We both win."

His cock slid in, then out again. His forearms, wiry with muscle, were propped on either side of her. With every thrust, his body rubbed her clit and his chest teased the points of her nipples. Sweat beaded on his forehead, and she sensed the tension inside him, the same as within herself.

"I don't know what you want," she gasped, frustrated.

He moved again, slower this time. Orgasm rippled through her, the first small spasms that would lead to a torrent of sensation, if only he'd move just…the right…way…

You can't give in order to get. You just have to give.

Tessa arched under him again. *You're already inside me, Magnus! What more can I give?*

"Yourself," came his whispered reply. His eyes flashed, twin green bolts of lightning. "I want you to give me yourself."

And all at once, Tessa understood. She had never held back her body, her sexual skills, or her business acumen. She'd never cheated her lovers or associates out of what she knew or what she could do.

But she had never, ever given anyone herself.

Her body still writhed and shuddered with desire, but now Tessa stopped straining toward the final peak. She looked into Magnus' eyes, really looked at him, the monster from her closet. Instead of digging her heels into his ass, she lifted her knees to pull him gently closer. She took his head, nestled into her shoulder, so he no longer had to support his entire weight on his hands. She stroked her palms down his back, lifted her hips, urged him toward the climax she felt building inside him…and she helped him find it instead of demanding he give it to her.

Magnus muttered her name in the curve of her shoulder, but she didn't know if he spoke it aloud or only thought it. It no longer mattered. She gave herself up to him. Everything she had.

He shuddered. His cock throbbed within her. He cried her name again, and her heart surged. Tessa opened her eyes to see his face, the green eyes shining and the blue sky becoming shadowed with night over his shoulder. The stars, like diamonds on black velvet, filled the expanse behind him.

They were floating.

And she was, too, Tessa realized. The long-awaited orgasm flowed through her, surging like the ocean, whispering like the wind, sliding like the sand, crashing like the waterfall, shivering like the snow. Then, finally, when she thought she could stand no more, when she must surely die from the ecstasy, the pleasure exploded and burst within her like the stars all around them.

Together, they drifted in space. Cradled in Magnus' arms, Tessa didn't worry about falling. After-shocks of pleasure rippled through her as he gave a few final, gentle thrusts, then lay still.

The softness of her own bed surrounded her, and Tessa blinked at the sight of her ceiling. She looked toward the window. Daylight streamed through the curtains. She looked at the clock, and muttered a curse, but couldn't muster the energy to get out of bed.

"I told you before," Magnus said mildly. "I can't *be* damned."

"Not you. The time. I missed my meeting. I'm late for work. My boss—" Tessa stopped when Magnus rolled off her and propped his head on one hand to stare at her. "My boss is going to be really mad."

"And?"

Tessa began to laugh. "And I don't care."

Magnus returned her smile and the sexy curve of his lips made her stomach flutter with erotic anticipation. "Ah."

"In fact," Tessa said as she rolled over to straddle him, "I've been thinking about a career change."

His hands came up to hold her hips. His cock, still unspent, twitched against her. "Really?"

Tessa leaned down to flick her tongue across his lips. "All I have to do is perform a seduction that creates a life change, right?"

He nodded and captured her head so she couldn't pull away. His tongue stroked hers before he murmured, "That's right. There are always plenty of openings for a good succubus."

Tessa wriggled her bare bottom against him and giggled when his penis lengthened. "Female version of an incubus, I'm guessing."

"Yes." Magnus slipped his hips a little higher, until his cock nudged her opening.

She sighed. "How soon will you know if you got the job?"

"I already know." He eased inside her. "I start immediately."

"And what about me?" Tessa breathed against his face. "When will I know?"

"That depends," Magnus replied. "On how long it takes for you to seduce me."

Then Tessa lost herself in his glowing green eyes, covered with his laughter, filled with his passion and cradled by the promise of a new life ahead of her.

MEGAN HART

Megan Hart began her writing career in grammar school when she plagiarized a short story by Ray Bradbury. She soon realized that making up her own stories was better than copying other people's, and she's been writing ever since.

Megan began writing short fantasy, horror and science fiction before graduating to novel-length romances. She's published in almost every genre of romantic fiction, including historical, contemporary, romantic suspense, romantic comedy, futuristic, fantasy and perhaps most notably, erotic. She also writes non-erotic fantasy and science fiction, as well as continuing to occasionally dabble in horror.

Megan's goal is to continue writing spicy, thrilling love stories with a twist. Her dream is to have a movie made of every one of her novels, starring herself as the heroine and Keanu Reeves as the hero. Megan lives in the deep, dark woods with her husband and two monsters…er…children.

Learn more about Megan by visiting her website…

http://www.meganhart.com

AMBER QUILL PRESS, LLC
THE GOLD STANDARD IN PUBLISHING

QUALITY BOOKS
IN BOTH PRINT AND ELECTRONIC FORMATS

ACTION/ADVENTURE	SUSPENSE/THRILLER
SCIENCE FICTION	PARANORMAL
MAINSTREAM	MYSTERY
FANTASY	EROTICA
ROMANCE	HORROR
HISTORICAL	WESTERN
YOUNG ADULT	NON-FICTION

AMBER QUILL PRESS, LLC
http://www.amberquill.com

Made in the USA